D0883671

APACHE RANSOM

Center Point
Large Print

Also by Will Henry and available from Center Point Large Print:

A Bullet for Billy the Kid
Frontier Fury
Chiricahua

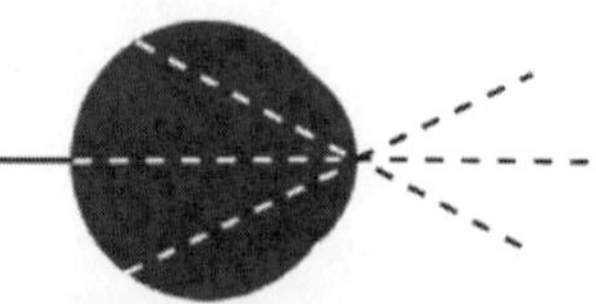

This Large Print Book carries the Seal of Approval of N.A.V.H.

APACHE RANSOM

Will Henry

CENTER POINT LARGE PRINT
THORNDIKE, MAINE

This Center Point Large Print edition is published
in the year 2016 by arrangement with
Golden West Literary Agency.

The text of this Large Print edition is unabridged.
In other aspects, this book may vary
from the original edition.
Printed in the United States of America
on permanent paper.
Set in 16-point Times New Roman type.

ISBN: 978-1-62899-875-7 (hardcover)
ISBN: 978-1-62899-879-5 (paperback)

Library of Congress Cataloging-in-Publication Data

Names: Henry, Will, 1912–1991, author.
Title: Apache ransom / Will Henry.
Description: Center Point Large Print edition. | Thorndike, Maine : Center Point Large Print, 2016. | ©1974
Identifiers: LCCN 2015044162| ISBN 9781628998757 (hardcover : alk. paper) | ISBN 9781628998795 (pbk. : alk. paper)
Subjects: LCSH: Apache Indians—Fiction. | Kidnapping—Fiction. | Large type books. | GSAFD: Western stories.
Classification: LCC PS3551.L393 A85 2016 | DDC 813/.54—dc23
LC record available at http://lccn.loc.gov/2015044162

To
EVE BALL

and to
Ysun's People—
the Apache of all Bands

Prologue

In the sacristy of a Roman priest in Ciudad Juárez, just over the line from El Paso, there is a document which should be of the historic record, but is not. Penned in old goose-quill script on stained vellum paper, it has the title *Narrative of Father Nunez*, and it was found beneath the vestry stones of an ancient chapel ruin in westernmost Chihuahua State, in October, 1933.

It is the basis of this book, which will begin, as Father Nunez's narrative begins, with this singular *dedicatoria*:

> I am Panfilo Alvar Nunez, once *cura* of the Mission of Saint Francis of Assisi, in Casas Grandes. Accept what I say, or deny it. There is no one else remaining alive to tell what happened.
>
> Had I been a Tejano, I would have died when the Tejanos died in their demented pursuit, casting for the mountain stronghold of the Nednhi Apache chief, Juh.
>
> But I am a Mexican, a *mestizo* of the *monte* in simple truth. That is to say, a man one-half of the Spanish and one-half of the Indian blood. So it was the Apaches permitted me to live, remembering my Indian mother.

It is a certainty that they will come back for me, nonetheless.

Apaches do not care for the truth to be known of them any better than do Anglos. But a priest of the people cannot shield evil.

Too many Tejanos perished on that terrible journey of vengeance.

There must be an accounting.

I give it here in this testimony to a man whose name will not be honored in his own land. If you can find it one time in any Anglo history book, I will lie to God about your confessions for all the days of your life. There is no risk to my vows in this: you will keep your sins and go to hell with them; you will never see the name of this man except that you see it here.

You may not see it even so.

Only God can know if these pages will endure. Revolt against Juárez is everywhere in the north. To the south, behind the fortress walls of the city, the old hero himself lies dying. Chihuahua is without defenses. Red barbarian, brown outlaw, white scalp hunter raven the very earth. Troops of the government hide like rabbits. Murderous *ruralista* bands menace all they happen upon. The poor and the decent pray for their lives.

Perhaps the truth itself shall die.

That it may not, I consign the name of the

tall Tejano from San Saba with my own name here beneath these vestry stones, asking of God only the little time to finish before the Apaches return.

It being His will, this narrative is inscribed to brave men of all faiths.

May I find my own courage, when I hear the fall of unshod pony hooves beyond my garden wall and look up to see the still, bronze face of Juh, warchief of all the Nednhis, watching me in that moment of the arrow's flight.

29 de Septiembre
Parroquia de la
Virgen de Guadalupe
Casas Grandes

Fr. P. Alvar Nunez
Order of the Monks
of Saint Francis

1

Of course one knows Casas Grandes.

It is the equal, nearly, of Fronteras or Bavispe or of Janos, even, as a legend-place of the Apache country. It has been on the maps of the *monte* since the Spanish came. Only look up there where the borders of Chihuahua and Sonora conjoin with the Arizona Territory. There it is. South, as the Apaches put it, "a two-day pony ride" from the United States. East, "but the look of an eye" from the centerbone of the great Sierra Madre, which the people of Juh call the Blue Mountains.

There it dwells beside the sparkling small river of its own name, the Rio Casas Grandes, itself a marker site in the history of Apacheria. Flowing out from the very foothills of Juh's forbidden stronghold, the river falls northward to end in the Laguna Guzman, midway to Ciudad Juárez. Its desert course watered the main Apache war-trail east of the Sierra, into the United States. It watered, as well, the beanfields, melon patches, and corn plots of Casas Grandes. Or it did on those blessed summers when God left enough flow within its shallow bed to reach our *acequias.* It was thus the artery of our lives; it was but an iron whim of Heaven—some say hell—that it also served the lives of the wild Apache.

Casas Grandes?

Ah! it might be the image of the blind poet's paradise, or the mirror of Gehenna's fiery pit; it depends upon the eye.

If one sees no beauty in glow of cactus orchid or bright halo of paloverde tree, for him Casas Grandes would be an ugliness. Did another, gazing westward over the grand rampart of the Sierra, behold only the blank stone of the earth's spine breaking free of the desert's crust, he too would cry an abomination upon the place.

For those of us who lived there in that singular time, Casas Grandes was an oasis of Christian hope in a solitude of barbarian death. A bastion, however frail, of God's house in a wilderness of heathen red horsemen and marauding outlaws of every wickedness. We clung to Casas Grandes as men who knew it was their last retreat, which they must defend from the Devil be he Apache *or* Anglo.

Casas Grandes was a true outpost. We were all soldiers who lived in it, all servants of the cross.

The mission was built in the seventeenth century by the Franciscans. A German friar supervised construction, demonstrating the plodding genius of his race. Even by that fateful spring when the Apaches came for the last time, the adobes had scarcely broken past their plaster coat, the ancient joists and sills of mountain oak were as sound as the day of their cutting in the nearby Sierra.

When I came to it in my turn, I was the nineteenth of its pastors in the Order of our Blessed Saint Francis of Assisi to serve it in unbroken line—a prideful thing for Church and priest alike.

Alas, we were not all children of the same forgiving God who came to Casas Grandes.

The final morning was of a kind to make the tasseled quail burst with song. The sun was everywhere within and without the mean hovels of the waking town. The people were in a glad spirit such as the Lord had fashioned the springtime to assure. Cactus wren, twit sparrow, ocotillo bird, and chaparral finch answered back the quail. All were likewise challenged by the reedy roosters of the village, each from his separate small mountain of cow chip or burro dung beside his master's dusty palace.

Quita! that sandpink dawn would make a pullet crow!

All cassocked and belted as I was, fresh from the early mass, I felt inspired to leap atop the mission wall and flap my arms to let God know his chanticleer could also cock-a-doodle-doo.

It demonstrates the original ignorance of man.

That was no pristine morning for Casas Grandes; it was a sunrise spoken of from that day in fearful whispering.

Its shadow fell first across my garden.

2

That moment is engraved in my spirit. One breath I was glorying in God's goodness; the next, I heard the soft swish in the sand of pony hooves moving up beyond the mission wall, and I knew *they* were there.

The wall rose perhaps four feet, framing thus only the upper bodies of man and mount. In the way that the eye will see all at a glance, I determined there were nineteen warriors in the band. That is, eighteen men and the leader. They sat, seventeen in the backing main pack, Juh in front, and on his flank a strange warrior whom I did not recognize. It was as my glance lingered on the strange Apache that I saw the twentieth rider.

He was no Apache.

Mounted behind the unknown warrior, his slight body had been obscured until he leaned outward to see what had halted the war party. When he saw me he made as though to cry out, as would be natural in such a small boy seeing his first civilized face in God knew how many pony rides from the place of his abduction. At once the handsome warrior struck him a backhanded blow, and the white child withdrew again behind his captor. I remarked at the time that he did not whimper or make any sound. I knew by this that they had had him some days at least.

Of course one could deduce this by the look of the party itself. The ponies were red with the sweated-on dust of far places. Faces and bodies of the riders were caked with grime. Even in these most impassive of nomad peoples, it was to be seen that the journey had been long and difficult and ridden at a killing pace. The dark faces were hollow with fatigue. The ordinary careful grooming of the Apache showed not in the nineteen riders who came to my wall. There was no question, even before Juh spoke, that this was a war raid party, that death was the twenty-first horseman who rode with them.

"Blackrobe," Juh said in that rumbling grizzly-bear voice I knew so well, "have the people prayed and gone away? We are in sore need of water and an hour to let the ponies breathe."

He spoke in Spanish, with Indian phrasing, a peculiarly Apachean speech familiar to all who might have intercourse with their fierce number. It was a patois I had myself mastered and now used in reply.

"Yes, Jefe," I told him. "The people have prayed and gone. No one is here. Enter and be as you would in your own camp."

"*Enjuh*," he growled, in his own guttural tongue, meaning "good." With the word he turned to his followers, waved, and repeated, "*enjuh, enjuh*," and the weary horsemen turned and came swiftly along the wall behind the mission. Here, on that side away from the town, was a portal gate wide and high enough to admit a single bent-over rider. I swung open the gate and the Nednhi raiders of the great Juh filed in with the speed and urgency of desert wild sheep driven to some rocky cul-de-sac of desperate need.

I soon learned the reality of this allusion.

My beloved mission was to become, in the space of fewer minutes than there were barbarian guests within its low ramparts, a fortress of Indian war.

My first understanding of this came with the thin far shrilling of a Mexican cavalry trumpet. I knew the sound and had not heard it within a twelve-month, or longer. Government troops were of a severe rarity in northwestern Chihuahua. "*Federales*," I said to Juh, and tucked my habit and ran for the wall.

I could see the command about three miles away across the flats to the southeast. The sun, being behind them, silhouetted them nicely. I thought I could comprehend, then, the urgency of Juh's weary company. The chief, unheard by me, had come up behind me.

"*Anh*, yes," the deep voice said, in Apache. "Huera planned it well."

"Huera?" I said. "Is that the new warrior?"

"*Anh*." Juh continued watching the oncoming

Mexican column. "Huera saw the trap in a dream."

"Trap?" I was at once alerted.

"There," Juh said, pointing to the left of the cavalry. "Squarely in the sun."

I saw the smaller dust cloud of a lesser band of horsemen bearing in on the mission. They rode a course converging with that of the *federale* riders. "*Quiénes son ellos*?" I said quickly, "who are they?"

"Texas Devils," rumbled Juh.

"What! Texas Rangers here?"

"*Anh*."

"After you, Jefe?"

"*Anh*, and now the Mexicans are after them."

"Huera's plan again?"

"*Anh*."

In my heart I did not like this. I grew wrathful but cautious, as one always must be with Apaches.

"Well, too bad," I said. "It is not going to work. The rangers will win to the mission before the Mexican cavalry. I will grant them sanctuary. Not even government soldiers will invade Church ground where sanctuary has been granted."

Juh uttered a grunt. Glancing at him, I saw the gargoyle's beak of his face break into what had to be a Nednhi grin. "We will help you give them sanctuary," he told me, and turned to order his fellows into place along the wall.

I remained with the Nednhi watching the

rangers and the cavalry come on apace. The feeling of a thing being terribly wrong grew within me. But the totality of the Apache chief's grim meaning was not to be conceived by even a *mestizo* mind, let alone that of a simple Franciscan *cura*.

The rangers, seven of them on flaming horses, won the race but narrowly—by the length of an arching rifle shot. Long Mexican lead was splashing the mission wall as I swung open the portal gate to admit the first of the gasping Texas horses. Busy with the heavy panel, anxious to swing it fast behind the last of the Texans, I did not see the horror that followed. I was yet shouldering shut the portal, all the rangers safely through it, when the earburst of point-blank rifle-fire thundered behind me.

As my heart leaped, the most dire fear that invaded it was that the Texans, riding with repeating rifles in hand, had instinctively begun to fire, seeing the Apaches dismounted in the mission courtyard. Would God this had been the tragic depth of it; it was not.

When the barking of the rifles ceased and I dared turn, I saw no pitiful scatter of Indian dead. Instead, where all had fallen within a circle of six *pasos*, the rangers lay riddled with Apache bullets. Even as I stared, paralyzed by disbelief, the Nednhi were over the bodies, smashing each in the face or back of the head, as scalping knives flashed to complete the coup de grâce by gunbutt. Sheer stupefaction rooted me. When finally I could force my limbs to act, I was barely in time to leap astride the last ranger body before the blood-spattered Nednhi had finished the other six.

The killing lust was in them and they came for me in a closing circle like the red wolves that they were. I had no belief—indeed, I had certain knowledge to the contrary—that they would respect the robe. There was, however, one whisper-thin chance. Seizing the cross girdled at my waist, I flung it up in their faces and cried out in the same instant, in their thick Apache tongue, the death word, *dah-eh-sah.*

The sun, by a grace of the Holy Ghost, struck the burnished silver of the crucifix. There was a burst of light in their slitted eyes and, as my cry of *death!* echoed, they paused the heartbeat needed for their great-chested leader to intervene.

Juh feared the cross. He knew it was the medicine of the blackrobes. Springing between his murderous pack and myself, he swung the butt of his rifle so as to knock the blade from the hand of the warrior Huera, who led the scalpers. As Huera cursed and stepped back, Juh said, to my amazement, "*Gouyan*, you are well named, a wise woman indeed."

A woman? This fiercest of the Nednhi pack? Then it was I knew that before me was a living legend, one of the near-mythical Apache warrior women. I knew also why my eyes had refused to leave the handsome young stranger among Juh's swarthy henchmen.

A priest is not by the mere fact of his devotions an empty vessel. He does not become, with ordainment, a gelded beast of the field. Indeed, I had experienced some persistent difficulty with this portion of the vows. The tantalizing bobble of a noble pair of breasts or the graceful sway of rounded young buttocks, whether well cloaked in village rebozo or covered by Apache buckskin pants, *pues*, *ay de mí*! they had never failed to send their signals to my guilty loins.

So it was from the first meeting with the warrior woman Huera.

I knew it, and she knew it.

But she broke her piercing return of my open stare to now fix Juh with a baleful glare, crouching as if to attack the Nednhi chief with the blade she had retrieved from the garden walk. It was a moment of real danger, for among the Apache the warrior woman is *ish-son kân*, god-woman, and considered holy. Yet Huera yielded as suddenly as she had cursed Juh. Turning without word for him or look for me, she fell to the Apache business of the massacre—the stripping of the dead enemy of arms and ammunition. In this work she was clearly the director, and even I could note the unusual urgency with which the Nednhi sprang to obey her bidding.

I thought I could understand that.

Each ranger wore two heavy Colt revolvers cross-belted at the waist. In addition, and far more excitative to the Apache, each carried a short repeating rifle of obvious new design. Huera directly bore one of these to where Juh and I stood, presenting it to the chief with a guttural comment in Apache. Juh nodded, dark eyes burning like pit coals beneath the deep overhang of his brow. He handed the rifle to me. "Here, Blackrobe," he said. "Look at this *besh-e-gar.* Have you ever seen one of its kind before?"

Besh-e-gar was rifle, and I took the weapon from Juh knowing instantly and even from my little knowledge of arms that not alone I but perhaps no one of the Chihuahuan *monte*, at least of Casas Grandes, had seen such a deadly weapon.

It resembled superficially the fine Henry Patent rifles that the Americans possessed in some number and which the Indians firmly believed could shoot all week from one loading. Indeed, some models of them would fire as many as sixteen of the short .44-caliber rounds they accepted. But this was no Henry rifle.

Peering at the deeply blued barrel, I saw upon it an unfamiliar name, *Winchester,* together with a date, 1866, not as recent as one would have expected but still, for our remote frontier, a new gun *de seguro.*

What dark portent that fact bore for me, and

for so many others then unknowing of their fates, will be seen.

For that moment Juh took back the shiny new rifle and lifted his thick shoulders almost in apology.

"We had to do it, you see, Blackrobe. We are out of ammunition, and we knew the Texas *Diablos* had these beautiful new guns and plenty of brass-cased ammunition for them. We killed three of them in an ambush when first they took our trail across the Rio Bravo, from Tejas."

"Texas," I said. "You struck in Texas?"

"*Anh*, along the stage road below the Cerro Alto but more toward El Paso del Norte, only a little ways out."

"God's Name! That is approaching the city itself? I cannot accept it. What brought you there, Jefe?"

"The boy," Juh grunted, moving his head to indicate the small white captive. "And these new guns. It is all a part of the plan, Blackrobe."

"You mean Huera's plan again?"

"No. Another's." The Nednhi chieftain paused, eyeing me. "Huera's plan was only to get these other seven new guns and shiny brass bullets for them. Since we had no more ammunition, she was leading the *diablos* to where we knew the *mejicanos* rode, where her scouts had sighted them and were leading them in a line to cross our trail and so the front of the *diablos*."

"Incredible."

"Nothing really. Huera knew the *diablos* would run for a place to fight from. Your church here was the only place. Huera said, 'We will get there first and when the *diablos* rush into the mission to fire on the *mejicanos*, we will kill them all and take their great new guns and kill all the *mejicanos*, also. That way there will be no one left alive to know that we have the guns, or where we go with them.' " Again Juh paused, again bent his craggy-browed gaze upon me. "That Huera is a devil herself. I am glad she is my virgin aunt and not some sister of the enemy. *Enjuh*!"

I objected feebly, protesting that here we were speaking of guns when the life of a white captive child was in direst peril. To this, Juh wrinkled the massive face once more in that red wolf's smirk that was a smile in Apacheland's view. "The boy and the guns go together, Blackrobe. Do I need to tell you that?"

He lost the grin instantly and I did not care for the look that replaced it. Fortunately, we were interrupted by the at-hand blaring of the Mexican cavalry bugler, and Juh was running for the walls with Huera and the others, levering the new Winchesters on the Apache lope.

Yet at the last possible moment, the warrior woman saw that the white child stood frightened and alone with the Apache horses. She veered from her race for the low ramparts, ran to the boy, seized his arm and, to my utter astonishment, dragged him to me. Thrusting him into my care, she said in Apache, "His life is your life, Black-robe," and she was gone.

But in that moment of the passing of the child, our eyes met.

I had not seen her so closely, nor with her riding headband thrown back. The eyes were not the snake's glitter black of her people. They were a golden hazel color, as of sunlit water pooling over desert sand. And her hair, released from the band, tumbled thick as ripened wheat, of a brown and glowing gold, over its Indian-dark undercolor. I was stunned.

She was what her name was.

Huera, the Blonde.

Certainly a Nednhi, or other Chiricahua-bred Indian woman in every feature of face and splendid form, she was yet a golden chestnut, even palomino, blonde. And she was, in that arm's-length exchange of the dirt-caked white boy, the most savagely exciting female of any race or complexion ever touched by this priest of the True Faith.

My guilty heart hammered, and not from fear of dying in the fight to come, or from cruel decision of Apache visitor, or even will of God. I was excited of that woman, racing yonder to kill my countrymen who thought to find but seven Texas Rangers within those mission walls. The smell of her, the look of her, the wildness radiating from her animal litheness, her cold Apache quickness to kill overcame all that lived beneath those Franciscan robes. I would never be the same priest again. Huera had looked at me.

It was in that numbed moment, before the crash of Apache rifles greeted the doomed Mexican cavalry and while the white boy clung to me in seeming mute fear, that I felt the grasp of another hand upon my habit's lower hem. I caught up my breathing as the tug came again—and yet again. *Nombre Dios*, could it be—?

Sweet Mary! Yes; my downward glance disclosed it: the seventh ranger was not dead.

3

In the tremor of time during which the stricken Tejano looked up into my face, I knew near-panic. An instinctual glance toward the south wall, where the Apaches waited with cocked rifles, showed the warrior woman Huera to be watching me. In the name of the Son why was she not, as her fellows, watching the Mexicans? Had she seen the ranger move to grasp my hem? To then clutch and tug so poignantly upon my robe? Raise his bloodied head to form the soundless words with which he pleaded for me to help him?

I could not know.

In that moment the lances of the Mexican riders flashed beyond the wall. The Apaches fired the new Winchester rifles in a rolling fusillade into the very faces of the blinded troops. Huera wheeled to add her weapon to the carnage. Hell took flame. The crashing of the Indian guns, the screams of dying men and animals outside the wall increased to bedlam. The Apache ponies began to mill and squeal. I stood clutching the stolen boy, mind addled with confusion. Not so the boy's quick intelligence.

"Say, Reverend," he advised, "you had best set me loose. We have got to give a hand to this here feller you're standing straddle of. He is surely bad hit and likewise is an old friend of mine. Let's ramble."

"Yes, yes," I agreed, freeing him. "Miracle of Jesus, you *know* this man? But wait. What does *ramble* mean?"

For reply, he seized the unconscious ranger by one leg. "Don't auger, pull!" he ordered me. "*Más aprisa*, damn it, Reverend. Grab aholdt that other leg!"

Restored by the boy's innocent valor, I grasped the free limb of the big Anglo. "Through the little iron gate, there," I panted, "into the mission burial plot—"

When we had the lanky body through the gate, I dropped my hold on it and told the boy to follow me. Together we reached the central headmarker.

Below this stone lay an ancient dry cistern converted by an earlier pastor into an Apache-proof sanctuary. Its secret had saved more than one shepherd of the Casas Grandes flock, and it was by Savior's Grace still intact in my time.

Prying up the large stone to reveal the dug-steps down into the gloom beneath, I ordered the boy to hold the heavy lid open, while I returned for the ranger. Like all small boys he was delighted at the prospect of an underground retreat, and he sprang to obey me with sprightly good will.

"I've got her, by cracky," he said, voice calm but blue eyes alight. "Shag on over yonder and fetch him."

Even as I seized the big Tejano's boots to haul him along the ground to the cistern's maw, I noted for memory the lad's keen intelligence and unbelievable lack of confusion or proper fear. Small wonder the Apaches had let him live. Smaller wonder yet that they had elected to take him with them and make of him one of their own. But there was yet another wonder coming.

I nearly burst open my groin pulling on that accursed ranger. He seemed to be all of seven feet tall and to weigh like a carcass of beef. By some gift of supernatural strength, however, I did get him to the cistern. There, as I strained to catapult him on down the waiting dirt stairpath below, he stirred. Coming to an elbow, he swept the gun-smoked courtyard in a single look, knew at once where fate had brought him.

"Padre," he said in pain, "you aim to hide a man out, you got to cover where you drug him from. Likewise, smokescreen the body count being one shy."

Here the captive boy broke in to pipe, "Hey, there, mister, you're late for the stage. But I knowed all along that you would easy catch up to it."

The bleeding Texan eyed him. "Thanks, kid," he groaned. "You are a grand help."

With that, he fainted, and I heaved him on down the steps into the cistern. The boy lowered shut the counterbalanced stone shell of the false tomb, and we faced one another across it. Again, he was quicker than I to recover. "Sure enough the gunfighter has got her pegged, Reverend," he advised me soberly. "We got to smooth out our tracks and rustle our butts into the bargain. The 'Paches just about got them Mexican soldiers of yourn nose-wiped. But don't worry, hear?"

The lad was right; both rate and return of the Indian fire were slowing. Only moments remained to us.

"Very well, *niño*," I conceded. "We shall pile the bodies of the rangers over the dragging marks, cover the pile with my holy robes and pray exceeding hard."

"I ain't much for hard praying, Reverend."

"Pray anyway. The Nednhis must not think to lift the poor cover to count the bodies."

"They're powerful smart," the urchin nodded. "But let's give her a go-round, anyhows."

And so we did.

With herculean labor abetted by the heavy drift of powdersmoke from the wall and the squealing and running of the now-stampeded Apache ponies back and forth in wild melee, we two made shift to pull the Texas dead all into a gruesome heap. Stripping my robe and vestments to white *pantalónes* and *guaraches* of Chihuahua mule leather, I cast the black shroud over the mutilated ranger corpses. As a final inspiration, I placed my belted cross atop the mute pile of bodies.

This proved not alone inspiration but salvation.

When we straightened and with pale haste stepped away to stand clear of our grisly cache, there was sudden, ominous stillness from the wall. Clearly we heard Juh's heavy voice.

"*Enjuh.* It is enough. Let them go; we cannot kill them all this time."

Next moment he and Huera had come to where the small Tejano boy and myself waited in vast unease.

"You did well, Blackrobe," Juh nodded. "No harm came to your charge." He inclined his massive head toward my valiant companion. "That's a valuable boy, hombre."

Huera said nothing but bent quickly to lift my robes from the dead Texans.

In the same instant, Juh saw the cross and commanded her to cease. She argued the order vehemently but I, in a unique visitation of good sense, announced somberly that if they disturbed these brave dead, the Tejanos would follow them on ghost ponies. "Who truly knows," I finished, making exaggerated sign of the cross, "what medicine powers such dead have? Seven is a particularly bad number anyway. You know that."

I did not have the least hazard that they knew seven to be a bad power number. Yet, Indianlike, they nodded gravely.

"Yes, of course we knew that," Juh said. "Come away, Huera. Leave the *diablos*. They died well."

The warrior woman dropped the hem of the robe.

"It is done," she told Juh. "Blackrobe," she said, turning to me, "you and I have our work now. And we need no ghosts to follow us. Go your way. *Enjuh*."

She departed then, taking the boy who seemed not to fear her. Juh swung at once upon me.

He asked if I had understood what the woman said. I was forced to answer that I had not gathered her true meaning, though I had heard the words plainly.

"I know that an Apache would never deceive," I lied to him, "but with a woman it is different."

Man-proud, Juh appreciated that. "She told you to go your way," he said, "because this time your way is her way."

I did not comprehend that either. I told Juh as much, speaking *a ciencia cierta*, most politely, of course. He responded in Apache kind.

"*Doble*," he said, "easy. Since you speak the tongue of the Tejanos, you are to be the messenger who takes the ransom paper to Texas. Huera will go with you."

"God's Name," I said in, a low voice. "What is this you say to me of ransom papers and Texas?"

Juh palmed dark hands. "He Who Has The Plan asked the Nednhi which man of Casas Grandes could talk with the Tejanos and might also be entrusted to make the long journey to the city of *el gobernador*. Huera, who advises us in such matters, named you."

"*El gobernador*, Jefe?" I strove mightily to be of outward complacency. "What service can a humble priest render the Nednhi by going to see the governor of Texas?"

Juh lost his easy way. His face grew at once dark with his old hatred of Texas and the Tejanos.

"He can tell him where his little son is, Blackrobe. And what will be the price of the boy's life, if he can pay it." He paused, bear's voice rumbling. "And he can tell *el gobernador* also what will be the length of his man-child's life if he, who is the boy's father, does *not* pay the price."

I took the blow well for a priest.

There is this game with Indians. They play it to make others lose poise, show consternation, become as the *mestizos* say, *muy chaveta*, very rattled. I knew the game. I did not permit my face to change.

But my heart betrayed me.

It pounded so fiercely within my breast as to smother the lungs with its beating.

What might I do now, what lie possibly tell implacable, brutal Juh, that would ease the shadow of Apache death hovering so near the impudent, undaunted Anglo boy whose young life lay in my hands?

4

The famed Nednhi stood silently waiting.

My mind was overwhelmed. How could the Apaches have made this bizarre stroke? To steal the son of the governor of Texas to hold for international ransom? No, never. This was the work of an *extraño*, an alien. An Apache mind would never conceive it.

"Very well," I said at last and carefully. "I am honored to serve the Nednhi. But I will need to see He Who Has The Plan. Let us go and speak with him."

Juh scowled and shook his head. Reaching into

his war bag, he brought forth a soiled envelope which he passed over to me. "That one has already spoken," he said. "His words are on the paper. Take it to *el gobernador, más aprisa. Entiende*?"

"Yes. But what then? When I have delivered the paper, Jefe?"

"I do not know. It is all on the paper."

"Is it permitted for me to examine the paper?"

"No."

"Who would know it, should I do so?"

"Huera, of course. She will be watching you."

"Ah, of course."

I knew that he had finished. Before he might leave I asked if I could go beyond the wall and tend the dying among the Mexican soldiers. He agreed, but said I would find none alive. I did not. The Apaches had shot them all through the head as they crawled about the ground wounded. I prayed over them as one man, for there were too many to count. As I did so, some of the Nednhis came out to get ammunition, canteens, swords, whatever of Apache use the Mexicans had on them. No sound came from these robbers of the dead, save for where a maimed horse yet breathed, struggled to rise, or kicked convulsively. These the Apaches killed by slitting the jugular. Ammunition was far too precious to waste on horses. But they loved horses and, cruel as they were to them in life, they said prayer words aloud for each one they released from pain.

A strange people.

When I had administered the common sacrament, I returned within the walls. Here, the Nednhi were preparing to depart. The last of the horses were being watered at the garden tank that was fed by wooden flume from my well in courtyard's center. Booty was being stowed, war bags tightened, saddles and bridles checked. Juh confronted me, as I hurried up.

"There has been a change," he said. "Huera will not leave the child. She says if the boy dies, the plan is dead with him. She will go on with us and with the boy. You will go alone to Texas."

I had been agonizing over the ranger hidden in the cistern and how I might treat him with the warrior woman by my side. Now the sun felt warmer on my face.

"*Enjuh*, Jefe." I saluted the big Apache. "Huera is as you say, a woman of rare wisdom."

"*Anh*, yes, and also one of keen eye," murmured a new, low voice behind me. "You do not fool me, Blackrobe."

It was the warrior woman, come up silently as we talked. I did not even wish to look at her she disturbed me so. But I brought myself to do it.

"Huera," I said to her, "we are both priests of our people. Will you not speak honestly with me? In what way do you think I seek to deceive you?"

"You know what way, Blackrobe," she answered.

"I don't like your power. I don't want to talk about it."

Strangely, she seemed afraid. At the very least she was highly nervous. Something had happened to put Huera on Apache edge. It was why she had decided not to stay with me. The boy's safety had been a false reason. The warrior woman simply wanted to be away and riding, to quit the mission and its undressed *cura.*

But Juh, too, had caught wind of her fear.

"What is this?" he accused her. "If the medicine to travel is bad, we will stay here for the night."

"No, no, we must not do that," objected Huera. "I wish to be far from here when dark falls. Come on."

"No," Juh growled. "What is the matter?"

Huera glanced around to be certain the other Apaches were out of hearing, not attending to our conference.

"Listen," she said, "they must not know. It would be a bad thing for them. They might do anything out of their fear. Even kill the boy, blaming him for it."

"For what?" demanded Juh angrily.

"Come," Huera said, low voiced. "I will show you."

We followed her, my heart bumping at the direction, straight to the grotesque heap of dead rangers. Halting, the warrior woman said to Juh, "Do you want to look under the blackrobe's coat, or will you believe what I tell you?" Juh shivered, shook his head. He would not touch that black garment, nor its guarding cross. "Very well," Huera nodded. "Believe it then, there are but six *diablos* under there. The big one, the last one that this blackrobe stood over to stop my knife, he is gone. How do you suppose he went?"

"You are certain?" Juh paled. "Absolutely?"

"Absolutely, yes. The big *diablo* is gone."

Juh sent his hawk's vision to stabbing every corner of the mission's inner space. He examined the earth about the pile of bodies, all without moving an inch. The running of the ponies had marked over every square foot of the courtyard. There was no hope to know by remaining sign what had happened to the seventh ranger.

"The church," he brightened desperately. "Surely that is it. He is in the church."

"No," Huera said. "I searched that place when I left you here to talk with the blackrobe."

"Where then?" frowned the Nednhi chief. "Are you saying that he vanished into the very sky?"

"Or beneath the earth," whispered the holy woman.

For a breath-stopping moment I believed she had seen me drag the Texan to the cistern. But Juh was on the plainer track.

"You are saying he is dead then?"

"Worse than that. This blackrobe spirited him away. He used his power to make him unseen.

There is no use at all to search for him. You cannot find a spirit. This place is cursed. We should burn it."

"Would that destroy the spirit?"

"Of a *diablo*, I am not certain."

"Well, then, we won't do it. Why hurt his church for no reason? Come on. I think there were only six of those *diablos* anyway."

"You know there were seven of them. We counted them every day for each of the days they have run us. Why are you trying to lie? *Chitón. Ugashe.*"

"All right," Juh said hurriedly. "*Ugashe*, let's go."

"*Enjuh*," the woman answered and went with the burly warchief of the Nednhi toward the saddled ponies waiting by the courtyard tank.

The last I saw of the Apaches, and of the small son of the governor of Texas, they were quirting their horses in a wide detour of Casas Grandes to strike the river beyond the town. Their dust cloud rolled briefly up the stream, faded in the first reaches of the roughlands rising to meet the great Sierra Madre.

5

When I reached the cistern and made a light with the prepared candle, I feared the Texan had died he lay so wan and still. But, praise God, he had only a bullet furrow in his dense Anglo skull. With a bit of camphor and acrid salts from the cistern's cache of medicaments, I soon had him restored. Hurriedly, I advised him of our situation. He immediately wanted to go above ground, but I persuaded him we must wait where we were in order to give the Apache time to be well up the Rio Casas Grandes.

"The while," I said, "tell me of yourself; we must have no secrets, Tejano." Fortunately, he agreed.

His name, he said, was Ben Allison. He came from the town and county of San Saba, in the state of Texas, where he had some ranchland and a small house on the drainage of the Rio Colorado of Texas. "Midway," as he explained it, "twixt Brady and Lampasas, and northerly of Cherokee about three days' drive." He was not a ranger, he surprised me by saying, but had joined the ill-fated company for good and grim reason of his own.

It developed that he, Allison, was in El Paso to buy a stallion for his ranch mares, but the sale had fallen through and, as he had planned to ride the stud home, he was left without a mount. Rather than buy a poor horse for the journey, he bought a ticket on the stage for San Angelo. It was at the stage depot that he met Henry Garnet Buckles III. The boy was there in the guardianship of his Mexican *dueña*, rather governess, who was also purchasing passage on the San Angelo stage for the boy and herself. The boy, taken by Allison's raffish apparel—the man was plainly a *pistolero*—had struck up a conversation with the tall San Saban, inquiring of him how was the best way for an interested young man to go about getting into the outlaw business.

While circling around that commitment, Allison had gotten from the lad his own most touching story.

The boy was in El Paso to visit his mother, who was ill in the army hospital at nearby Fort Bliss. He had said good-bye to her that same day, he and the governess returning to town to await next day's early stage.

He did not believe, the boy said, that his mother was improving as she insisted she was. Still, she had smiled many times, repeatedly assuring him she would be home in the spring, and he must tell his daddy so.

Here, the Mexican governess had taken the San Saban aside. The lad's mother, she confided, was gravely ill of the lung fever. She had come to the post hospital because of the army's experience with the disease. But the *medicos* had failed. She had perhaps but days remaining. The boy, *por supuesto*, knew none of this.

Allison thanked the woman. He returned to the boy and bid him to take heart and believe what his mother told him. He then promised to see the lad on the stage next day, saying he had meanwhile another journey to make, which was private.

It was to visit the mother at the post hospital.

In their young days the boy's mother and Ben Allison's sister, Stella Allison, had been closest girlhood friends. Then Stella had been declared missing in the great Brownsville Raid of the Mexican freebooter Cheno Cortinas. Ben and his brother Clinton had not seen Mary Anna McCulloch—the mother's maiden name—through all the years since that tragedy, not even when she married the governor and sent them a genuine printed invitation to the State House. Now Ben knew it was long beyond that time, and he must go and talk with Mary Anna McCulloch.

The woman wept to see the tall brother of her olden friend. Ben, no creature of iron, could not prevent the shaking of his own voice, nor the answering tear. He hid both, he thought, at least enough not to add to Mary Anna's burden. When he could, he asked her about the boy, whom she called Little Buck, after his father, known throughout the Southwest as Big Buck. In turn, she wanted to know if any word had ever come as to the whereabouts, or fate, of Stella Allison. When all of this gathering of the old times had been sifted through, the tall Texan said, he and the woman had come to it. As a ranch girl would, Mary Anna put it straight to the mark and did not, again in Allison's twangy words, "go wide around the rough spot."

"I am going to die, Ben," she told him. "You must not let Little Buck know this, but if you can do it, I would pray that you take the stage with him and see he gets home to his daddy. If you could see Big Buck, tell him his Mary loves him and asks he forgive her for keeping the secret of, well, you know what I'm saying to you—the way that it is going to be."

At this point, memory rose up in the tall San Saban so strongly as to interrupt his narrative. When he had rallied himself, he concluded in the strange pattern of the Tejano dialect.

"Padre," he resumed, "that was a mean hand to play, leaving that poor woman. I told her that, by God, she was not agoing to die and that, yes, Christ Jesus, I would vow to shelter Little Buck back to the capital, and she could close her eyes on that and rest easier than a bay filly with her nose in the oat bag. Last I seen of her she was smiling and waving me a Comanche farewell sign I had taught her as a kid."

Again, the big man had to wait, again resumed

when he could, the words tightening beneath the Tejano drawl.

"Well, Padre, that was a long night awaiting for the stage to leave come sunrise. So I wandered out on the town, had me some Old Crow bourbon whiskey, enough to leach out the last sense in my pea-gravel brains, and wound up acrost the river in Ciudad Juárez, skunk-drunk and snoring it off in a Mexican whorehouse.

"When I got back over the Rio, the sun was three hours high and the San Angelo stage was fifteen miles out and rolling east at a six-horse clip.

"I done what I could. I knowed where the fastest horse in them parts was, and I went and got him. Didn't have time to discuss the price. Didn't figure it to do no good anyhow, as they wouldn't sell him to me the day afore. So I merely stole the son of a bitch and took out after the stage."

I had to laugh, here, even as a man of God.

This lean, fierce-looking Anglo was a passing odd and quaint fellow. He had a sort of sun shining within himself, which illuminated his view of things even when events were dire. In this case, he nodded his understanding of my levity—that it was not an ignoring of the sorrow in his tale—and finished quickly.

He said that, about six miles out of El Paso, he had come upon ten rangers quartering in off the prairie from up by Cerro Alto mountain. They were running a hot track and a bad rumor. Some friendly Lipan Apaches had told them that Juh had been camped in the nearby Tinaja Pintas for several days. The Nednhi chief had with him a band of what the Lipans called "bad" Indians—known raiders and haters of the Tejanos—riding out of the Mexican Sierra Madre Mountains. More, and worse news, Juh had boasted he would soon be the "biggest man" of all the Chiricahuan "four families." Since this number would include such as Cochise and the original "pure" Chiricahua; old Nana and famed Victorio of the Warm Springs Chiricahua; and young Geronimo of the intractable Bedonkohe Chiricahua, the boast was strong medicine.

Of course it was known that Juh was addicted to some even stronger medicine—the raw and gut-rotting whiskey of the Pinda Lickoyi, the White Eyes. As a legendary drunkard, even by Apache standards, Juh's talk had to be watered down severely. It remained a fearful claim: the Mexican Nednhi Chiricahua were in Texas to carry off the only and small son of Governor Henry Buckles, then known to be visiting his bedridden mother in the post hospital at Fort Bliss.

The ranger troop had been on its way to El Paso, after a three-day scout up from Jeff Davis County, to check the rumor and to mount guard over the youth if anything were found. North of El Paso, they had struck the trail of a sizable band of hostiles heading due-line to cut the stage road east of that city. Knowing the San Angelo run would be rolling that morning, they had swung east to intercept it and turn it back until they had "chaperoned" the Apache war party safely across the Rio Grande.

It was at this point that my tall patient's memory once more constricted his throat. He went on to the bitter ending only with difficulty.

"It was right then, Padre, that I had to break in on the ranger captain and tell him his coach was an hour early leaving El Paso, and we was already seven, eight miles behind it. I asked and got permission to ride with them, and we put the hooks to our ponies clean into the shanks. It was maybe an hour later, nearing high noon, that we seen the smoke ahead.

"You know what we found. All dead but the boy, and him only figured to be alive because there wasn't no body for him in the wreckage of the burning coach. The captain sent one man back to El Paso to report the massacre, and the rest of us cinched up and whipped on. We wasn't more than thirty minutes back of the Apache and they knowed it. We damn near got them at the river, then again down past Guadalupe and Bravos, on the Mexican side. We hung on. The captain was determined to do or die.

"He made it the bad way.

"The bastards set us a trap in the salt cedar

brakes of the Santa Maria. Got Captain Caldwell and two men down and the rest of us had to fort up under a sandbank. Had to watch them beat in the heads of all three—still alive—and ride on out free as chaparral cocks.

"That was yesterday, sundown. We lost them by dark and gambled on a blind stab for Casas Grandes, as the Lipans said that Juh's bunch come from the Sierra back of here. We was praying we could beat them to their hometrail and waylay them like they done us.

"You seen what happened.

"Your damn bugle-tootling Mex cavalry jumped us four mile out and it was 'run for the river, ranger,' all over again. The onliest stream we could see was yonder dry wash, so we hit for your blackbird corral here on the hill. We never seen the Apache this morning, until we seen them inside your churchyard."

The San Saban drew a final, long breath.

He looked upward, into the gloom of the cistern's stairwell. "God help and keep all you Texas boys laying dead up yonder," he said, in that arid, soft voice I was to remember so keenly. "And all them sungrinner horse soldiers, too, I reckon."

Then, the soft voice honed to an edge of knife-steel. The pale gray eyes turned to blaze upon me.

"And Christ Jesus give me the gut-strength, Padre, to trail up and kill every last one of them Apaches of yourn that was here this day."

6

I looked at the big Tejano, startled. It was a fearsome oath that he swore. Moreover, it failed of touching the true heart of the hour's tragedy. "God forgive you," I cried. "You speak of death for the many, rather than of life for the one. You have forgotten the boy!"

"Sure I have, Padre," he said, getting unsteadily to his feet. "Come along on and guide me out'n this hole before I forget what I promised his mama, too."

"Ah, *dispénseme*, hombre; I wronged you."

"You ain't the first by several hundred," he told me. "Lead on."

We went quickly up the stairway. At the top, I felt for and found the lifting crevice in the hollowed gravestone. Raising the stone an inch or two, I peered out. As quickly, I lowered it again.

"My people are already out there," I said. "They are up from Casas Grandes to pay their respects to the dead. That is, to rob them of the last ring and trinket as they pray over them. Then perhaps, when they remember it, to look to see if their beloved priest still lives. But I must not reveal the secret of this vault. Come at once. There is another way. *Cuidado, hijo mío.* Do not bump your wounded head."

We went, bent double, by the alternate dark warren, a small tunnel hand dug by slave Indians long since and safely in Christian graves. The passageway led under the church itself to surface in the confessional. Arrived there, I went up first. As I well knew to expect, my *pobrecitos* were more morbid than repentant; the church stood empty. "*Más aprisa*!" I whispered down to the waiting Texan. "All is well."

We reached my study without incident of discovery.

Here, I belatedly attended his head wound, binding it with a stout bandage to impede the flow of blood. Allison proved more impatient than grateful.

We had, he insisted, really to put a twist in our tails as the Indians had hell's own start on us.

To this, I answered *we? us?* and asked if he dreamed that Father Alvar Nunez would think to ride with him after the savage Nednhi? I suggested the bullet had burrowed nearer to his brain than seemed apparent.

Ignoring me, he demanded to know whether I commanded the use of any good horses. I of course did not, but I informed him that I did hold ownership to a fine riding mule. At this, he first took the name of the Savior in vain, then inquired if my animal were jack or jenny. When I replied neither, but a hinny, he asked, in evident Anglo humor, if perchance she had a sister. I was able to bring him up short by advising that she did indeed, being one of a set of splendidly matched twins, the other of which was the property of Bustamante, *alcalde* of Casas Grandes.

Being a stockman he understood a hinny to be the offspring of a stallion horse to a she-ass, rather than the reverse, usual mating of jackass to mare horse in producing mules. The hinny to my knowledge was smaller, of more spirit and greater cunning than the common mule. It had been the riding mount choice of Chihauhuan and Sonoran since the Spanish came, and we *mestizos* swore by its virtues.

Allison in any case had no choice.

I had seen his big American *entero*, studhorse, sail high over mission wall at outbreak of the rifle firing to disappear into the outer battlesmoke. The brute had gone with saddle, bridle, and booted Texas rifle, and I now told its owner as much.

It became his turn to confound me.

It might work out just fine, he said. His Comanche Indian kinfolk had taught him that hinny mules, being nonbreeder hybrids, made excellent horse-stealing mounts. They did not get horsey, as she-mules did, and would go right into enemy camp or horse herd without bringing or giving equine challenge. "Leave us go and borrow Bustamante's twin to yours," he finished. "You can make it up to him in free baptizings and buryings."

In vain I tried reason on him.

I was not going with him on any manner of mount, or for any distance farther than the bean-fields of Casas Grandes. The Nednhi band of the Chiricahua Apaches was justifiably held to be the wildest of all the four Chiricahua families. Juh knew me and respected me as a holy man of my people; he even feared the cross as unknown medicine. But he would kill me as quickly as any other *mestizo* of the *monte*, should I be so insane as to guide, or even go with, a white Tejano into the Sierra looking for him or the Nednhi strong-hold.

The Texan admitted this was precisely what he had in view. He would remind me, however, that as a holy man of my people, I had more than Juh and the Nednhi to concern my conscience. One more, in fact. His name was Henry Garnet Buckles III, and he was only eight years of age. Was it not a fact, Allison challenged me, that Juh had put the life of the boy in my personal charge? Or had I lied about that part of our situation there at *Misión de la Virgen de Guadalupe*, near Casas Grandes, that morning of the glorious spring?

Not giving me time to reply, he remembered something forgotten in the stress of our journey from the cistern.

"Say," he rasped, "let me see that there ransom note, Padre. It may give us a set of tracks to guide on. Or leastways a hint of where we are at."

I was as guilty as he of forgetting the document. More so, *de seguro*, for I had received it from Juh's own hand. Yet, bringing it forth from waistband of *pantalónes*, I remembered something else about it; it was sealed.

"We cannot open it," I said. "Juh warned me."

"He didn't warn me, Padre; hand it over."

I still demurred, apprising him of the Nednhi's threat that any tampering with the ransom words of He Who Has The Plan would endanger, if not cost, the life of the small captive.

Allison looked at me.

It was a gaze to wither a prickly-pear stem.

"Padre," he said, pronouncing it *padry* in his irritating cowpen Spanish, "Padre, you ain't telling me that the pope in Rome don't teach you fellers how to unstick a letter and glue it back together again. Huh! That'd be like a Texas rustler saying he couldn't change nor put back a brand. Hell, you got to have some kind of running iron to get along in your business, same as any of us."

There was no further use to deny him.

Ben Allison had not been conceived in his mother's womb to be denied.

Yet I continued to stare him down.

Was I not a priest of the True Faith, and he but an ordinary being?

7

Some of the trueness of my True Faith wavered.

Allison stood six and a half feet in his high-heeled Texas boots. He was wide and square of shoulder, lean in hip, flat of muscled belly, menacing of demeanor. The eyes were *lobo* eyes, pale as wheat straw. The sun-bleached shag of hair, horse-sheared at the back, escaped flat low crown of black Stetson hat as a lion's tawny mane, yet the color of his skin was Indian dark.

Indeed, he was bowlegged and pigeon-toed as any red man, and, shrinking now under his burning gaze, I recalled his passing mention of the Comanche tribe of Texas.

I determined to secure the requirements.

So, with certain skilled heating and other recourses of deceivement, the document was opened. Spreading its sole page where light of candle might fall across it, the San Saban and I bent low. Our indrawn breaths came as one at what we saw.

Hon. Gov. Buckles
and Texas Military

Is it no use to think of recovering the boy. The captors, who will be the new people of

North Mexico, are not yet reliable. They understand this much at least—they know what the ransom is and desire its payment fiercely.

The terms are these:

1. Surrender and delivery in exchange boy's life, all small arms and ammunitions to suit, Arsenal United States Army, Post of El Paso.
2. Single messenger to come to the sender from governor bearing acceptance of terms and authority to arrange exchanges.
3. No public's knowledge.

Any carelessness will kill boy in certainty.

I looked up and met the Texan's eyes across the candle's fitful light. To my interest, he appeared to have read the document as swiftly as I. But then it was in English, his own tongue and not mine.

"*Por Dios*," I murmured. "What do you make of it?"

It was not, the wolf-eyed Texan told me, what he made of it but rather what I did. He *knew* what he was going to do. The same as before. Go after Juh and get the boy back. Kill as many Apaches in the process as God would let him. And do it *más pronto*.

"Nothing ain't changed," he said. "Dicker or no dicker, they will kill the kid. Ransom notes from hostile Injuns might as well be wrote on bung fodder, for what they're worth."

"But God's Name!" I protested. "The governor must know of the note. He must see it, even as Juh ordered. You cannot take this terrible risk upon yourself."

"Padre, you coming or staying?"

He started for the study door, and I blocked his way, entreating him to be sane. If he did not wish to trust the Apaches, then think of the *lunático* who had planned the El Paso raid by the Nednhi. The one who wrote the note was plainly an educated man, almost of a surety an Anglo. He was of a certainty no Mexican or Indian. And, of whatever race, his mind was frighteningly that of a false messiah. He clearly dreamed to establish in Chihuahua and, little doubt, Sonora, a barbarian nation of armed Apaches. The ransom note said as much.

"*Hijo*!" I cried out to him. "We have a madman here!"

Allison gently placed both of his hands on my narrow shoulders. The fingers, the size and hardness of desert mesquite burls, sank into my flesh.

"Padre, why you think I'm carting you along? You're the case-ace chance there is to get anybody white into that Apache camp. Without we do that, we don't nail us this *loco grande* or get near the kid, neither one. Now you got a count of three to make up your mind, or I'm going to hoist you up and hang you on yonder hatrack."

I did not care to be hoisted.

Moreover, in his salt-cured Texan manner, he had shrunk the business down to its true dimension—the life of an innocent child.

"There is no other way?" I parleyed desperately.

He shook his head. There were, he said, two things guaranteed to happen provided the governor of Texas and the commanding officer at Fort Bliss received and understood the contents of the ransom note: both very bad.

First, the governor would send the single man as messenger, all right. Decoy messenger. Behind him would stalk whatever number of rangers, or other volunteers of Indian-killing credentials to pass muster as pedigreed Apache chasers, as thought needed for the job; the job being the wiping out of the Nednhi.

Second, the army commander would send a bogus string of canvas-tarped wagons to look like the demanded load of small arms and ammunition along down to whatever rendezvous was subsequently set. Then, when the Indians came in to get the guns, they would find them at the shoulders of U.S. troops and again get wiped out.

There was not, the tall San Saban concluded,

one man in Texas out of ten hundred that thought they knew Indians, and *did* know them. The sole reason he himself might be gambled on as an exception was that his maternal grandmother had been a full-blood Kwahadi Water Horse Comanche, and blood sister, also, of the sinister chief, Peta Nocono, father of fabled Quanah Parker.

He had, the big man said, lived as many years with the Comanche as with the white man.

He knew the ways both thought.

And in this case the way that the white men would think would, sure as the sunset, kill Little Buck.

He knew, too, he added at the last, the ways of the Texas Rangers. They were brave as wounded bear-dogs in any fight, could whip up to ten times their own number of any other breed of man, Apache or Mexican.

That's what made them so especially dangerous to Little Buck Buckles.

If Governor Big Buck Buckles and the C.O. out at Fort Bliss both somehow managed to consternate Ben Allison and obeyed the ransom note to the dots over every single *i,* the rangers would still get the captive boy killed by forcing for the Apache stronghold on their own.

"Ain't nine of them already died to prove it?" the big Tejano finished. "You want that poor little kid to make it ten?"

I did not, *por supuesto.*

In some way Ben Allison's quiet, pale-eyed words had reached me. Made me feel more of an *hombre del monte* than a soft-bodied priest. And I must confess it, may Jesus forgive me, they had put me once more, and hotly, to thinking of the supple woman Huera.

"*Tiene razón, usted,*" I told him, "you are right."

Then, a welling of human adventure rising in me as nothing else I had ever experienced of the flesh, "Let us go and see Bustamante—!"

8

The twinlike devotion, one to the other, of the two hinny mules made our work easier. Since they would not bear separation, both were kept in the livery barn of Alcalde Bustamente. If either the mayor or myself wished to ride, the other hinny went along as pack animal or simply running free as a pet dog might.

When I explained this to Allison, he grunted that he wished to God we were at home, in Texas, where a man could steal himself a couple of good horses and be on his way without all this nonsense of creeping around the back side of the town to come at Bustamante's stable without the villagers seeing us.

However, he granted that in the present case it was best that it not be commonly advertised what we were about. In fact, he advised me, as we lay hidden in the deep arroyo at town's edge behind the livery yard, it would be an even better idea not to let Bustamante himself know of our plans for his half of the twin hinny contract.

When I inquired with priestly indignation if he were suggesting we steal the mayor's mule, he protested as offendedly that, no, he certainly was not suggesting it—he was about to arrange it.

And so it went.

In the broad, bright light of midmorning, that most improbable of tall Tejanos spirited both hinnies out of the livery stalls of Bustamante's barn and into the Arroyo Casas Grandes behind that structure without bringing solitary village cur to yap or nosy settlement urchin to stumble upon the outrage. *Chispas*! he was beyond any question a premier *cuatrero*, a supreme horse thief; yet, hold, one must be fair to Providence.

It is also true that no Anglo of common sort, one without Comanche blood, could have done the thing unaided. Nor could Ben Allison have brought it to pass, either, except that, through my presence, he had the help of God.

Still, he plagued the mind to wonder.

From the barn of Bustamante, also, in the less than ten full minutes that he was gone—while I skulked in the sage of the arroyo—the big Texan, to use his own term, "borrowed" bridles, saddle pads, surcingles, and a valuable horsehair riata, or throwing rope.

In addition, he entered the main *casa*, stole the food from Bustamante's table, a large jug of the mayor's private *aguardiente*, two villainous-looking scabbard knives, and, munificence of Mary! Bustamante's prized and ancient revolver, a memento of the Texas Ranger battlefield at Matamoros, on the far ocean coast of Tamaulipas State.

This rusted weapon, Allison assured me, was itself worth the entire risk of our levy upon the house of Bustamante. It was, he said, a genuine Walker Colt. It came fully charged of cylinder and accompanied by the proper belt pouches of cap, ball, and powder. If it would discharge when triggered, the Texan vowed, he and I alone might start a new Mexican war—and win it!

Such esprit was a contagion.

The man contaminated me from the outset with his impossible optimism and incorruptible simplicity of belief that, where men were in the right, they could not fail.

I had thought myself well armed with my own faith, but Ben Allison's clear-eyed credo outmarched it that day. When we had stolen safely past the town and were five miles away up the river trail into the mountains, pausing to look back and down upon my beloved mission outside

Casas Grandes, I understood the first hint of my former error of belief.

The theft of the two small mules was a laying on of Ben Allison hands.

God had very little to do with it.

9

At the five-mile halt, Allison took a pair of soft buckskin *n'deh b'keh*, Apache Moccasin boots from the booty-sack of things stolen from Bustamante. Where indeed the *alcalde* of Casas Grandes had come by these items was less the wonder than that the big Tejano had found them in his lightning raid of the mayor's *casa.* He seemed always to be guided by some mind less simple than his own, this tall man from San Saba. Again and again, I was to see him demonstrate this absolute gift, but never was I given to understand it. If not my God, then some spirit *kân* of his Comanche ancestors certainly rode beside him. He himself saw it as but another article of his peculiar faith. "The Lord helps them as helps themselves," he would shrug. "Let's mosey."

Donning the Apache boots, now, he cinched up the great Walker Colt about his waist, took a good long pull at Bustamante's jug, passed same to me. "Drink up, Padre," he said, scanning the ascent ahead. “She’s going to be steeper than a slate roof.” To my astonishment, he took back the jug, poured some of the fiery liquid in his palm, and gave each of our mules a snifter. The perverse brutes dumbfounded me by sucking noisily and smacking rubbery lips for more. “Never knew a Mexican jackass didn’t take to gardente,” he nodded. “Specially if there ain’t no mescal.”

We went on, climbing steadily. The river was far below now, on our right. The walls of the first rampart of the Sierra yawned before us. Our way was by a goat track suspended on the sheer face of a plunging cliff. In places it bulged beyond the perpendicular to literally lean out over the canyon of the Casas Grandes. I had never been this far, having come only to the five-mile turnout below. But the Apaches had traveled it for three hundred years. Even I, a soft man of the villages, could follow the hoof-channeled path of the centuries. As for Allison, he soothed my fears of the increasingly dizzy heights by assuring me that, wherever a “redass Apache” might go, a quarter-bred Kwahadi could “hang with him easy.”

When I objected this was fine for him but did not include in its guarantee a bent-backed priest of Saint Francis, not even one whose own-mother had been an Opata Indian of these same northern Sierras, he proved equally helpful.

“Hmmm,” he said. “Never knew no half-breed

priests. Howsomever, it don't matter. Some of the best folks around are half-breeds."

"*Gracias*, hombre. And I have even known some good Anglos. Even some good Tejanos."

"Why, sure you have, Padre. Bastards ain't all whelped out of the same stray bitch."

"A verity of the ages," I agreed. "Excuse me now, I need the breath for climbing."

The Apache "road" was pitching upward acutely. In places we perforce dismounted and went afoot, the little mules following like mountain sheep. For the main, however, they strove valiantly to bear their riders without such charities of dismounting. It was in their heritage. They were *mulas de España*, Spanish she-mules, proud blood, but mortal all the same.

The Texan was so tall he continually put this or the other bootsole to the ground to assist his mount, Jugada, Mean Trick, in the climbing. This could not fail of embarrassing the poor thing, but she did not falter. My own animal, Lata, Tin Can, bearing a small man of God who towered four feet and eleven inches, the blessing of a humpen spine from birth, suffered no such humbling.

Up and up we went. The hours, and the day, fled.

The clifftops pulled in together above us, the great crack in the mountain—the Grand Canyon of the Casas Grandes—yawned black as the pit below. In those times when we halted to rest the mules, the silence was fearful. In it, we could hear the whispering of the river a thousand feet beneath us. It was an ethereal sound, stirring the soul, arousing something I could not name from deep within me. Near the top, I made mention of the feeling to my companion. He nodded at once.

"It's your Injun blood. Makes you feel like you'd been a place you never was. Ain't that it?"

That was, of course, precisely it.

Impressed anew with his strange gift of seeing and feeling things beyond my educated ken, I questioned him closely in this case.

"I don't rightly know, Padre," he said. "Injun blood ain't the same as any other. It's old blood, and wild. Carries things in it to put pictures in your mind, just like they was printed in a book. Yet it skips, too. Some don't get it. My brother Clint never had an Injun thought. Me, I been Injun-hunchy and spooky-wild since I was a kid and could remember. It's more like I was three-quarters Kwahadi than one."

I agreed with him. He walked, thought, and looked like a Comanche Indian. It was only the pale, tawny hair and wolfish eyes and the arid Tejano drawl of speech that marked him an Anglo. He even had an Indian sense of humor I thought: wry, sly, outrageous, self-effacing, bawdy, yet always quick to sober, or turn sensitive.

We remounted and began the final ascent of half a thousand feet to the topping out of the cliff trail at the brink of the ancient Nednhi Falls. I shivered, feeling the blood of my Opata mother. Spurring the tiny Tin Can, I kept her as close behind tall Ben Allison as her sister hinny, Mean Trick, would permit. Casas Grandes was another world and three hundred years away. Beyond the Nednhi Falls, even God did not go. Beyond the Nednhi Falls, the Apache waited.

10

We broke out suddenly upon a high Sierran bench, or flat, and I thanked God that the cliff trail was behind.

The rock-strewn level before us held a wild, lonely beauty. Blue juniper, dwarf cedar, red-limbed madroño, and aromatic mountain scrub of the high country softened the jumble of great and small boulders that littered the flat and hid, from our view, the continuance of the trail and, of course, any Apache horsemen upon it.

The Texan held up a warning hand, and we reined in our mounts, listening, in a parklike scatter of silver-trunked trembling ash saplings. Of animal or bird life we saw and heard none, a certain sign, Allison told me, that the Apache had passed but minutes before us.

To our immediate right, the river went over the lower cliff in that roaring outleap of green water known to us Casas Grandeans as the Nednhi Falls, although not appearing as any falls, whatever, on the Spanish maps. Inward of falls' brink, the stream tamed to placid meadow brook, looping in grassy course back through outcrop of stone and straggle of tree to where lay the fabled Old Campground of the Chiricahua people.

It was here, Juh had once told me, that the four families met historically. Old Campground was the intersecting place of two great Apache trails. The first, called South Way, went down five days' travel below Casas Grandes, to Pa-gotzin-kay, the so-called Apache stronghold of the Bedonkohe, Warm Springs, and True Chiricahua bands. The second trail, West Way, trended west by north two days' journey across the high divide of the Sierra Madre to Cañon Avariento, the secret entering cleft to the Nednhi band's retreat. This retreat, called by us Juh's Stronghold, was continually confused by both Mexican and American "authorities," with Pa-gotzin-kay.

All of this local information I called out above the thunder of the waters to an attentive Ben Allison; and I was proud to be able to at last contribute something of value to our adventure.

When I had done, he motioned me to follow him away from the falls. Under a rocky overhang, we dismounted. Here, the Texan got down the *aguardiente* jug of Bustamante and rationed each of the mules another palmful of the fiery liquor.

They muzzled it up with shameful pleasure, as though the *alcalde* and the *cura* of Casas Grandes had weaned them on the evil fluid. Allison freed them to trot away and fall to grazing in a nearby, hock-deep stand of mountain clover. He beamed with admiration of the small brutes, that is, as much as his dark and narrow face could beam. Turning to me, he nodded, "Damndest critters ever I see," literally the second words he had uttered since starting up the last, terrible ascent of the cliff trail. He then pulled me in under the overhang with him, handed me the jug, and said, "Better have one, Padre. It's apt to be a long night."

He fell at once to work; I watched him, fascinated.

What he was doing, he said, was testing our artillery here and now where the sound of the falls would cover the necessary small noise. Spreading the recharging gear of Bustamante's ancient Colt revolver, he first put several of the ignition caps on a stone and struck them smartly with the weapon's steel butt strap. Four of the five caps so smitten "cracked" their tiny explosions faithfully. The fifth fizzled and smoked out. "Not too bad," he said. Next he poured three mounds of powder, one from each of the three pouches on Bustamante's belt. Two of the three piles flared nicely when lit. The third smoldered noxiously but did not ignite. He discarded the guilty pouch. "Cuts down our supply," he said, "but boosts our odds."

He next removed the old charges from the cylinder of the revolver, discarding them also. With the weapon empty, he worked the trigger mechanism, blunting the fall of the spurred hammer with his left thumb. Satisfied, he stood up and belted on the holster with the gun in it. I did not see what happened then, but by some motion I found I was one instant looking at the big weapon in its carrier and next instant seeing it in Allison's hand. I blinked and he said, in his drawling way, "God, it don't pull like my old Army Model, Padre, but you can pray a lot for me."

"Ahhh," I said, in a long manner, almost accusingly, "you *are* a *pistolero*."

He shook his head, denying it.

"Never was," he said softly. "Folks say things that ain't so. Then they get to believing them."

With that, he placed inside his shirt one of the two vicious Mexican blades stolen from Bustamante's house, proffering the second knife to me.

"Got to carry some kind of medicine, Padre," he nodded.

"What?" I said, refusing the blade.

"You forgot your cross," he answered.

By habit, I clutched for my crucifix. It was not there; it was back guarding the dead rangers in the Mission of the Virgin of Guadalupe. I had brought away from my quarters a spare robe and cowl to don when we were safely away from Casas Grandes, but of second *cruz* I had none. Indeed, to that moment, I had verily forgotten my priest-hood.

I forgot it still.

"Give me the knife," I said, the voice not even my own.

He passed the evil-looking steel again.

"Hide it, Padre," he ordered. "They're not likely to look for a *cuchillo* on a father. We may need that edge."

"I could never use it, hombre!"

"You don't know what you could do, Padre."

"I could never kill!"

"It's an old tune," said Ben Allison. "I've heard it whistled in many a dark place."

"God is with us," I told him. "Be of high faith."

The Texan looked at me. The lean head bobbed. The pale eyes sought me out.

"Sure," he said. "Meanwhile, carry a good knife."

He went on quickly. We were less than one mile from the cross-bench rampart that marked the second uplift of the range. If his eye read the lay of the benchflat correctly, the Apache meeting of trails, hence the ancient campground, lay about midway of the distance to the uplift. Half a mile, he said, maybe less. This factor, taken with the lateness of the day—the sun was gone, the mountain twilight falling swiftly—narrowed our choices to two.

We could bed down where we were, giving them the next morning to clear out, following them at a respectful remove and hoping to somehow "catch them careless," and so free the boy and make our run with him.

We could otherwise go on in under cover of the presently gathering dusk, get into the rocks as near to them as possible, figure to make our strike for the boy in the deep dark of night, gambling everything on Ben Allison's ability to "Comanche sneak" the sleeping Nednhi camp and "lift" the white boy safely from it.

I had the natural-born Mexican right, the Texan concluded soberly, since we were in my country, to vote my preference in any way that seemed fair to me. To this I agreed, asking him, however, if there were not some possible additional options, not so chanceful.

To my relief, he answered that there were, and again they were two in number.

I could go home either by the way we had just come or by the way we would both go, if the Apaches caught us. To which I at once responded, "And what way is that?"

"Why," he said, as quickly, "by the river, and baldheaded."

I shuddered. The vision of my barbered corpse

floating out of the Sierra with the next high water of the Rio Casas Grandes did not appeal.

"Very well," I surrendered. "What is 'our' vote?"

He hesitated, peering in his wolflike way across the silent bench to where we could now see the first risings of the Nednhis' campsmoke. "Injuns can vanish just like that fire smoke," he said softly. "We wait for day, we might never see this bunch again. Nor the boy alive, ever." Again the pause, the pale eyes burning.

"We'll go in tonight," he said. "Now."

11

We lay in the rocks above Old Campground, I, at least, grateful to Providence that we had reached the vantage undetected. Below us was the Laguna de Luz, the legendary Pool of Light, in the Rio Casas Grandes, midway of the mountain bench. Owing to some peculiarity of light sand bottom and water clear as the air about it, the enchanted lakelet gave forth a luminescent glow, even in the approaching darkness. Its beach, inland of the Nednhi drop-off, was smoothly sanded, perfect for the tribal bathing that now went forward in the quickly made Apache camp.

The behavior of the Indians was that of happiness to come again where only the Apache trod and where the grime, and even blood, of the trail's long riding might be laved away. All the warriors and most of the horses were either in the pool or moving into it. Two of the band's number, Huera and the captive Anglo boy, were to be seen making their ways about the shore of the pool, away from the men.

Glancing at Allison, quiet at my elbow, I noted that he was watching the advancing pair with a frown.

I reassured him. It was the Apache custom, I explained in some vanity of knowledge, for the sexes to disrobe and bathe separately. Here, the woman, Huera was only bound on this mission of modesty and not on some venture boding ill for her small charge.

The Texan's frown deepened. "A woman, Padre?"

"Forgive it, yes. I forgot to tell you. The one coming with the boy is Huera, a warrior woman."

"My God," breathed Allison.

"See there," I whispered back. "She will not leave the boy but that she has selected a place of privacy for herself beforehand. Not even with a male child will the Nednhi women expose themselves. Ah, see—!"

Here, my companion gripped my arm in a bear's trap of sinewy fingers. "*Callate*," he whispered.

I obeyed. It was that, or lose the arm's use. Huera had halted directly below us. Here, the beach narrowed to a band of rocky shoreline only. The woman indicated to the boy his small inlet. He understood and quite gladly began removing his clothing. Huera, waiting only to see him so obey her, stepped on along the narrow shore and around a screening boulder. We could see this place even better than that of the boy. Again, I had cause to admire Allison's skills in the stalk. He had so placed us that we could see not only the beach and the men opposite, but in effect command the whole of the pool's irregular and rock-scarped basin. Yet we were invisible from any view of theirs. But then of course I had to recall that he was part Comanche Indian, a fierce, fierce people of the highest arts in the hunt as in war.

I looked at the big Tejano, now, with this affirming thought in mind, smiling to show him my appreciation. He mistook my motive. "Why, Padre," he whispered, "how dast you!"

The reproval was so plain, in both small murmur and pantomime of gesture, that I glanced guiltily below.

The woman was standing there naked as the day of her delivery, except for her calf-high *n'deh b'keh*, her rakish Apache boots. Even as the blood thickened in my temples, she stooped gracefully to discard these last remaining garments. In the action, her rear was upended in our direction, not once but two times. I saw, even if fleetingly and in failing light, the parts of a woman I had never seen before. *"God In Heaven!"* I breathed. "I am choking."

Allison set his jaw and put finger to lips, admonishing me to silence.

I turned back to the sinful view below and, thank God, the woman was in the water.

I felt the Texan's bony elbow in my ribs.

"You watch the boy," he mouthed to me. "I'll take care of her."

I glared at him, offended. But he grinned and leered at me, and what might a man of the cloth do when guilty as was I of panting after forbidden fruits?

I put eye to Little Buck, where the lad splashed and made noises in the water seeming no more in alarm than if in some swimming hole of his homeland. I presumed that the Texan was brute-like in his opposite vigil, and I could envision his animal looks and lickings of evil lips in hunger of the marvelous body disporting on his side of the partition-rock.

Even so, I was able to pray for strength and to find sufficient restored faith to see the entire moment for the grand vista of barbarian beauty and peace that it truly was. It was while I was yet so purifying thought and directing unruly eye toward the cross-pool beach and the good-humored calling back and forth of the Nednhi men bathing there, that the first rifle shot rang out. Its startling, alien crash was instantly echoed by the terrifying snarl of many other rifles from the rough terrain behind the white sand beach.

Ambush!

And every Apache man in the water away from his weapon. With a woman and a captive white child isolated on pool's far side, trapped there and helpless.

I started to my feet but Allison seized me with one long reach, literally throwing me to the ground.

"Stay down, damn you! We got no chance!"

Neither did the poor Nednhi.

There was never a question of battle but only of escape. A man does not count bodies in an instant of that frightful nature. Yet one knew that nearly half of Juh's force did not gain free of the water. What the eye did record was that, in the Apache fashion of war rules, the men fled with no attempt to reach or defend the lone woman with them. As the hidden rifles continued to stab forth the orchid stamens of their deadly nighttime blooming, perhaps ten or twelve of the surprised war party found bare back of pony and rode out of the trap at Old Campground. These survivors, Juh among them, went by South Way. They had to. The ambushers lay in the rocks cutting off West Way and the trail to home. In less than four minutes, the riflefire fell away.

In the stillness that followed, the killers came trickling out of the rocks beyond Pool of Light.

One by one, they came down to the fires lit by the Nednhi to broil the evening's horse meat. As the leap of the flames carried illumination to their faces, I felt the long body of the Tejano stiffen by my side, and I heard his indrawn curse.

"Whites—!"

Then, swiftly, "Oh, Christ Jesus, no."

"Do you know them?" I whispered, horror numbing me.

"It's Kifer," he said.

The name needed no amplification for a *mestizo* of that Mexican time and place. Nor for a priest of the people. It was a name not alone born, but bred, in infamy. A monstrous, loathsome, hell's broth of a name.

Santiago Kifer.

The own and only son of the renegade American scalp hunter of the generation gone, Dutch John Kifer, who, through all of the terrible years of the 1840's, hunted down and pelted Indians of all tribes, in Chihuahua and Sonora. An Apache scalp in those noisome days brought two hundred and more dollars, and legend had it that the elder Kifer had made upwards of a hundred thousand American dollars in a single year of his reign of hideousness.

Recently, within the past two summers, only, the officials in Ciudad Chihuahua had once more begun to pay for "Apache hair," and the whelp of the old wolf had appeared to follow the awful hunting of his sire throughout the Sierra Madre of the North.

The mention of the name, now, was a blasphemy.

"*No, el Espíritu Santo no quiera*!" I cried, in suppressed whisper. "God forbid it!"

"If He did," Allison murmured grimly, "Kifer didn't pay Him no heed. That's the son of a bitch yonder, and by my count there's ten men with him. All Texicans, you can bet."

Kifer was Texas-bred, known to hire only the best of Indian hunters. In working rule, this usually meant only other Tejanos. Even the Apache feared the Texas men, most probably because of the fierceness of the Texas Rangers in their warfare against the red man. And here was the dreaded Santiago Kifer, with a big band of Texas scalp hunters, only a few *pasos* away, around the margins of Laguna de Luz.

In first panic of the ambush, I had forgotten Huera and Little Buck. The Apache woman, when I belatedly looked to find her, was disappeared from the water, either having dived beneath some shoreline rock-shelf or having left the pool to seek hiding in the boulders below us. But the Anglo boy was still visible, and he was out of the pool and running along the south shore calling out to the men he had seen attack the Apache camp.

Of course! Dear Jesu, of course!

Were they not white men?

Had they not come against the Indians with flaming guns and from perfect ambush?

And could not his lonely young heart hear the message those twanging drawls brought to his ears, as the Texans moved in about the Nednhi fires?

What other possible thought could invade the imagination of Little Buck but that the vengeful minions of his father had somehow caught up with his abductors and that he was then as good as on his way home to his father and his poor ailing mother. He had only to reach the white heroes beyond the pool and reveal to them they had found and saved the son of the governor of all Texas.

"God Amighty," I heard Ben Allison mutter beside me.

With his oath, I was again to my feet. And his big fist was again knotted in my robe and slamming me flat to rock-hard ground.

"You jump up on me one more time," he rasped, "I'm going to cave in the side of your skull, you hear me?"

I nodded, but was still desperate.

Where was the woman?

Ought we not to look to her safety, if the boy were in no danger?

No and no were his terse answers.

The woman was a red Indian. Naked or not,

she could look out for herself. As to the boy being in no danger from Kifer and his wolf pack, nothing could be further from the truth. The moment he told them who he was, up went the Apache price for his life.

Santiago Kifer was wanted for murder in every Texas county west of Fort Worth.

He had nothing to lose by holding the boy for blood money. Christ knew, if he had to, Kifer would sell Little Buck back to the Apache faster than he would give him up, free, to Governor Buckles or the state of Texas.

"But they won't harm him none, meanwhile," he concluded. "And the Injun woman's safe away into the rocks without they ever knowed she was part of Juh's bunch. So we just lay low till some-thing breaks open."

We had not the time to settle ourselves to his advice, when the something broke.

And devastatingly into the open.

It was the warrior woman, Huera; she had circled the pool in the rocks above Little Buck to get ahead of the running boy, and she came now down out of those rocks, in full view of the scalper pack on the white sand beach.

To a man they saw her.

The superb pagan nudeness of her body gleamed for that fatal instant in the water-refracted red light of the Apache fires. Then she had seized the boy and, like some mountain lioness of lithe bronze, bounded with him back into the cover of the scarp-rock.

She was too late and forever too late.

With a chorus of ugly cries, the Texas scalp hunters were after her.

12

Ben Allison was gone from my side in the instant that the Apache woman, Huera, revealed herself to the scalp hunters. Terror seized me. God in Heaven, had he deserted us? Sweet Mary! what a coward's truth—all that a man hath will he give for his own life. I was abandoned, with Huera and the boy—my only chance to cower where the Texan had left me and to pray that Santiago Kifer and his ugly vultures would be circling elsewhere when the dawn came.

But the brave small boy? And Huera, lovely slim Huera? I could not desert this twain. They were of my own blood, each of them. Jesus be with me, I must go to them.

As I rose up from my hiding place, the scalper pack closed on Huera in the rocks of the south margin, dragging her down to the sanded beach. Two of them had Little Buck, fighting and twisting like a catamount cub. Never believe that the human beast does not snap and growl. The men of Santiago Kifer were upon Huera as mad animals, attempting to mount her two and three at the same time. The sound of their snarling was that of brutes. Untutored as I was, I knew they would kill her with their fornicatings. A virgin as she must be, in her holiness among the Nednhi, she would have no experience of coupling by which she might reduce the woundings of repeated entrances. She would die there on the sand, while they yet ravaged her.

Bounding down from my rocks, I raced along the pool's track to reach the lust-mad pack. Drawing close, I heard Huera softly moaning and I could see that she lay nearly still. With a blind oath, I hurled myself upon her attackers. But one of them felled me instantly with a boot into my manhood. Then another struck me below the heart. And a third balled oaken fist to pit of my stomach, shot bony knee upward beneath my chin as I fought to rise up yet again.

I lay stunned, senses dimming.

It was then Allison came out of the rocks behind the Apache camp, slashing as a lean wolf against the scalp hunters where that obscene pack yet humped and crawled above the groaning Nednhi woman.

He came among them in total silence.

The great Walker Colt revolver was in his hand but he did not fire it. He struck with its steel butt into the heads of the men on Huera, lifting and heaving aside their slumping bodies in the same motion with his free left hand. So swift, so completely startling was the attack, that four of the men lay about on the beach, heads bleeding, before the remainder of the pack might rally to come up behind the Texan.

Even so, he got to the fifth man, the one beneath the others. And this was the one he meant to kill. The great gun was jammed into the man's very face, where Allison had pulled him up from his straddling of the now motionless Huera. *"Kifer,"* the arid voice said in the softness of death, *"God damn your soul."* The hammer fell in that moment, the Walker roared its fiery response, enveloping the scalper's head with its point-blank flame.

Yet God, or Satan, relented of the vengeance.

Kifer, twisting violently aside in the instant of the discharge, was not killed.

The gun's burst, but a hand's length from his face, burned him black with powder-spew and waddage. Yet the deadly leaden slug itself, although it carried away the upper half of the right ear, failed of its lethal aim.

In the eye-flick of time wherein Ben Allison understood this—knew that he had missed—the remainder of the scalp hunter pack was upon him from the rear.

The final belief I carried into my own unconsciousness was that they had surely killed him.

13

When senses returned, I was wise enough to remain motionless where I lay, commanding the blur of my vision to steady. It was then I saw the carnage from the raping of Huera spread upon the beach about me. Nausea whelmed me. I nearly vomited into the sand.

The Nednhi men murdered from ambush had been brought ashore, and their hair had been taken by the scalpers. The tops of their heads showed a grayish white of gristle and skull sac, bringing another wave of illness within me. A single blessing obtained; there were but five of them, a mercy of God compared to the greater number I had thought to see slain.

Near me lay Ben Allison. Beyond him, poor hand seeming to reach for his in mute testimony, was the warrior woman Huera. The limbs of both appeared bent in the unnatural postures of departed life. I saw no movement of breath in either form. The Texan was a cake of blood about the head and face from the merciless beating of the scalpers. The bullet furrow of his original injury had been ripped wide and bled a puddle the size of a pottery jar lid beneath the wheaten mane of his hair. Huera had bled heavily, also, but in a lower place; I wept the salten tears of silence to see her so, a broken thing, a child's Apache doll, left in the long trail of her people's sorrow.

I thought then, belatedly, of Little Buck. But nowhere in the view I had of the beach did I see the Texas lad.

Not far off, the scalp hunters were gathered about the one tiny fire yet burning. They were in heated, tense discussion. Some of the human reasons for their anxiety lay in the sand just past their guarded council fire.

Two men, either dead or comatose from the terrible damage of Ben Allison's revolver butt, were stretched full-length and unmoving. A third man was lying with them doubled up in a knot and whimpering like a wagon-crushed dog, his hands groping for his belly in spasmodic agony: the victim of the bullet intended to blow away the head of Santiago Kifer. And then there were yet two more men sickeningly lacerated about the skulls by the Texan's pistol steel. They were crudely bandaged and propped up against their saddles; one of them babbled in a manner to show that it would be the greater tragedy should he survive—the brain was gone—he mewed and cried as a suckling baby. Again, I nearly puked upon the beach, but did not.

Somehow, God brought it into my still dazed mind that death would come should I show life. It was already miracle enough that, due to the pitch of their fireside discussion, they had not been alerted by my recovery. As I waited, feigning that same broken sprawl as my poor comrades, this truth was borne starkly to my slit-closed eyes.

The man who had been struck in the bowel began to cry like an animal. Kifer came up off his haunches by the fire and was at the man's side in a single long pace. He knelt, I thought to minister to his henchman's need. But it was a ministry of darkness. I heard the fellow's gasp and the ensuing gurgle and bubbling, and I judged these to be the sounds of drinking from a held canteen. They were not. Kifer had cut the man's throat to still him.

That was not the obscene sum.

Wiping his blade, the pack leader started his return to the fire. The man with the ruined brain reached to tug aimlessly at Kifer's pantleg, making animal sounds. "Charley," I heard the monster say, "you don't know nothing, do you?" Again, he knelt, but not to use the knife. His hand felt for and found a stone of melon's size. I could hear the sodden pounding in of the frontal bones. The baby's mewing stopped.

"Jess," he said to the third man, "you going to be able to ride?" He had the rock in his hand, poised to strike again. But the man, Jess, answered yes quickly enough and thanked Kifer for tending to the others, for quieting them. Kifer dropped the rock. "Sure," he grunted and went on to the fire.

"We got two dead yonder and two more going to die quiet," he reported. "By using their horses to ride relay, we can make it on into Casas Grandes before them 'Paches change their minds. They quit too easy on us."

"They did for certain," said a swarthy, pot-bellied man. "That was Juh's own bunch. Them Nednhi are hell."

"They'll shadder us account the squaw," Kifer muttered. "When I was ramming it into her, she kept crying *ish-son kân*, *ish-son kân*, but I didn't catch it then."

"Christ," the potbellied lieutenant said, "they'll dog us sure."

"Yep," another agreed. "Never knowed them to leave a holy woman with whites."

Kifer hitched at his pants. To my dismay, I saw that he was buttoning up. He had not even taken the decency to cover himself since the terrible thing he had done. "Catch up the horses," he said. "Kick out the fire. Ketchum—"

A bone-thin scalper lounged around the fire while a third man scattered the remaining brands of its bed.

"Yo," he answered, in the manner I had heard American cavalrymen use. "Whereaway?"

"Go yonder," Kifer rasped, pointing to Allison, Huera and me. "Slit the gullets of them three. *Más pronto.*"

"Too bad," laughed Ketchum, unsheathing his

blade, "ain't none of them got good black hair. Mebbeso, I'll take the squaw's anyhows. Might be they'll pay double for a yeller-pelt Injun. Ha, ha."

Kifer leaped after him. "You touch that squaw, I'll sell *your* hair in Ciudad Chihuahua, damn you. Ain't I just said she's *ish-son kân*?"

Ketchum uttered an obscenity. "Sure didn't look it when you was astride of her," he grinned. "Funny how holy she's got all of a suddent."

Santiago Kifer just laughed. It jarred the ear, a sound of strangely unsettling timbre. There was a feel of insanity to it, a madman's low, formless mirth.

Ketchum understood its wordless menace.

He came quickly away from his companion, looming in the inky gloom nearly upon me before I might rally brain and hand, or two good legs, to serve the purpose of my own escape. In the heart-beat intervening, I saw another movement, even nearer me, that put forever from my mind the lure of selfish flight.

Beyond the body of Ben Allison, the hand of Huera moved—I saw it clearly and heard in the same final instant a soft sound from her, as moaning.

Ketchum stepped over me to come first at the Nednhi squaw. A lifetime for God went out of me in the primal urge that blinded me. Unknowing, by an instinct old upon this earth before ever Christ of Nazareth drew breath, my hand found itself inside my robe. I was on my feet soundless as the Angel of Death, who in sudden fact I was. The Mexican knife of Bustamante given me by tall Ben Allison went into the bent-down back of the scalper Ketchum as his own blade touched Huera's stirring throat. May God forgive me, I put it to the hilt in him, ripped it upward through the greater muscle of his dorsum, and cut the heart's very sac.

He was dead in the one strangling gasp.

Over where the fire's embers winked lastly out on the sand, Santiago Kifer, already to horse, reined his frightened mount around.

"Ketchum," he called, low voiced, "*qué pasa*?"

Off in the higher rocks of other mountains southward, a wolf cried lonesomely, sobbingly.

No other answer came to Santiago Kifer's call.

"Jesus!" the potbellied man said. "Let's get shut of here." The others, crowding their horses into his, gave wordless mutter of agreement.

Kifer knew the smell of death as few men did.

He drew it now into his nostrils and heeled his mount away from the stench growing at Old Campground.

"All right," he said. "Ride out—!"

14

To dispel the darkness of spirit and flesh, I lit a new fire on the beach at Old Campground. The pack of Santiago Kifer would not return that night. If the red wolves of Juh did so, well, a priest still had his vows. All four of the wounded with me—Allison, Huera, and the two scalpers abandoned by their mates—had recovered consciousness and required aid. A man of God could not deny them. Such skills as were mine and what power of prayer I possessed would alike be used for the murderers as for those they had tried to murder. God would understand it if, in the while, I cared first for Huera and the Texan.

Allison, from first splash of cold pool water on his battered face, came swiftly back. With that remarkable skull of his, thick as any Nubian's, he was again more bloody than beaten. Within five minutes of regained senses, he was on his feet helping me with the others.

We could do little for Huera. We cleansed her with fresh water and the Texan made a tea of strongly boiled mountain fescue and an alpine weed I did not know but which he said was cousin to an herb the Comanche used as astringent and antiseptic agent. It had power, this I saw, for when he laved it gently over the tortured parts of the Nednhi woman, she cried out in hurt and, only moments later, opened her eyes for the first time.

Within another few minutes, the bleeding below had slowed and, before long, stopped altogether. "Now," Allison said, "if she don't get infected, she will likely make it. Happen she don't meanwhile sull up on us, she will."

"Sull up?" I asked. "*Qué significa* sull?"

"Well, Padre," he said, holding the Apache woman close to him to stop her trembling, "it's like what a wild horse does when he cain't get free, or has broke a leg and knows he's caught. He will just stand there and take to shaking, then pitch over dead. Sometimes there ain't a mark on them. They die anyways."

I had studied in the Franciscan Academy of Medicine, in Valdosta. One in so many frontier priests were so prepared. Now I nodded to the Texan, understanding.

"It is called *choque*, Tejano. The systems of the body diffuse. The blood depresses. The heart stops."

"You got to keep them warm," he told me. "Pass me over two more of them Nednhi blankets yonder. Steep some of that tea we brung along from Bustamante's. *Más aprisa*, Padre. She's looking to sull on me; I can feel her heart tugging. God damn it—"

He took Huera by the shoulders, shook her

sharply. Putting his mouth to hers, he blew his breath into her. Then he shook her again and put his lips to her ear.

"You hear me, little Injun?" he said, in English. "*Schicho*, I'm your friend. *Hoh-shuh*, *hoh-shuh*, easy now. We'll guard you. You're safe with us. But I want you to stop that shaking. *Hoh-shuh*, little sister. Do you hear my words?"

There was a moment when I feared the darkest thing.

But presently the closed eyes reopened, the lips moved, and I heard the words, "*Anh*, yes, I hear you, brother," and, unbelievably, her violent shivering diminished and she murmured, "*Enjuh*, it is warmer now."

Allison patted her like a child, wrapped about her the blankets that I brought, laid her carefully by the fire's warmth. "*Enjuh*, *enjuh*," he said. "No harm is here. We are your friends, sister."

She lay back, breathing eased, faint color replacing the ashen gray of her skin. I knew the immediate peril was suspended. I caught the Texan's eye.

"That was a remarkable thing you did," I said.

"Sometimes a hurt thing will gentle," he answered, "other times not. Depends if they believe you."

"She did then, Tejano, for she lives."

He only nodded and looked around the deserted beach.

“Where’s the boy?” he asked. “You got him safe-hid somewheres?”

“He’s gone. The men that had him must have let go of him to join the ones beating you to the earth. I pray that when they thought to look for him, he had vanished into the rocks. But I have called to him with no reply.” I paused, shaking my head, glancing apprehensively up into the shadowed boulders of the south margin. “I fear greatly that he, too, may be crouching up there in the state of mute fear, sulling, as you say. He was witness to horror.”

Allison refused the thought. “Not him,” he said. “He ain’t the kind to sull. That kid has got more gall than a grizzly bear’s bladder. He’ll show up, providing Kifer ain’t got him.”

He looked past me to where the wounded scalpers were at last sitting up. “Maybe they was the two had Little Buck,” he said. “I’d best find out before they go under.”

I told him I doubted the men were in danger of dying. “Just as you, hombre,” I concluded, “they have heads of stone, rather than bone.”

“You’re a poet and don’t know it,” he answered. “Stay by the squaw. Get some of that tea down her.”

Glad enough, I remained with Huera. I was still tending her when I saw Allison coming from beyond the fire. “*Cuidado*, Padre,” he said. “The ’Paches are back.”

He was supporting the two befuddled scalp hunters and, as I strained to see the returning Indians, he sat the pair against a boulder behind me, warning them to say nothing and to behave as though too ill to understand anything. “The padre’s got a pull with the chief,” he added. “He’ll maybe be able to mumbo jumbo them into leaving you be.” One of the men, a beardless young brigand, not unhandsome, thanked Allison. The other, an older and vicious-looking fellow, merely nodded. He seemed to know the quality of the mercy he might expect from the Nednhi. “Remember,” Allison said, “*chitón*!”

It was a Spanish expression of the *monte*, meaning, “be mum.” Both men nodded agreement and lay back.

With growing unease, I returned my gaze to the outer darkness. Again, I saw and heard nothing, absolutely. On the verge of angrily reproving Allison, for no man of that country cared to hear the word Apache spoken carelessly, I saved my lecture. In the last of the rocks reached by our fire’s feeble light, there came a hint of movement. Then followed the dry click of unshod hooves striking trail stone. Ghostly horsemen materialized, seeming to emerge from the very marge of Laguna de Luz. Thirteen of them, halting now to sit in slant-eyed silence, just beyond the fire.

Juh, and the twelve surviving Nednhi.

Come back for Huera, the Blonde.

Even in the uncertain drama of the moment, I wondered at the instincts of the tall Tejano. How had Ben Allison known those shadow horsemen were inbound to our fire, when I had no warning of their approach?

Was it that "wild" thing in the Indian blood, of which he had told me?

And, if it was, would the Nednhi return the feeling; would they know, by their own instincts, that Allison was a quarter-brother of the blood?

It did not seem so in the first of it.

After an interminable stillness, during which Juh and the others examined the entire visible range of the beach, the fire's proximity, and all within it, a single handsign was made by Juh to the braves in the rear of the immediate group flanking him.

There was a grunting of assent, a stir to make way among the foremost ponies. Up from the rear of the savage troop rode two warriors leading a captured horse between them. Astride this animal, his feet tied beneath its belly with buckskin thongs, an Apache headband gagging small Anglo mouth, was, *por supuesto*, the urchin son of the governor of all Texas.

"Praise God, Jefe," I said to Juh, "I make you the Sign of the Cross."

Although his impassive, broad face showed no least flicker of emotion, I knew he was pleased. As has been said, he believed in the power of the medicine in the *cruz* of the blackrobes. "*Un-nuh*," he nodded, which, in Apache, signified approval without praise or permission.

All of the Nednhi now dismounted.

Allison stood where he was, not moving except to breathe. The two bloody-headed scalp hunters pressed back against their boulder, white not from their wounds alone. Beneath my hand, Huera made a soft sound and sufficient movement for the Apache to note. Juh turned to me. "She will live?" he asked. He knew of my reputation in medicine. Often enough, the Nednhi had brought their seriously wounded to me at Mission of the Virgin, in Casas Grandes. On more than one hard-pressed retreat, such gravely hurt fellows had been left in hiding with me while the band fled on into the Sierra Madre. Once, even, Juh had taken me to Janos, there to treat the great Mangas Coloradas, himself, when the Gila chieftain had been nearly killed in an Anglo trap. So these fierce *bárbaros* now listened, and leaned with Juh, to near my answer for their holy woman.

"We think that she will," I told him carefully.

"We?" Juh said.

I pointed to the Texan. "Yes, the Tejano saved her life, Jefe. It was not me."

"You lie, *jorobado*!"

When angry with me, Juh would use that word, "humpback," rather than to call me Blackrobe. So I took warning.

Stooping, I drew a large cross in the white sand of the beach. I then made a circle around the cross and stepped within the circle. "I am within *la casa de la cruz.* No man of my faith lies while standing in the House of the Cross. I say it again, Jefe. The Tejano saved Huera."

Juh was a huge man for an Apache. Indeed, for any race. He moved toward the Texan and his eyes were level with those of the very tall man from San Saba. "How are you called?" he asked.

"Allison," the Texan answered laconically.

Juh's nod was scarcely perceptible.

"*Un-nuh,*" he said.

He stalked past the Tejano, his men following him. They made a wordless half-circle about the two wounded scalp hunters. They just stood and looked at the helpless whites, saying nothing either to them or among themselves. "Black-robe," Juh called to me, "what of these?"

"They will also live."

"*Enjuh,*" the Nednhi chief announced to my total surprise, "good. I would not want them to die now."

Allison looked at me, and I at him.

"Injuns—!" he said and shook his head.

The Apaches then moved with the precision typical of their desert people. While some of the warriors gathered booty left behind by the fleeing scalpers, others put the bodies of the Apache dead in preparation for burial. At the same time, a detail, with a camp shovel found among the scalper prizes, commenced to dig two deep holes in the beach sand. I presumed these were for a group interment of the Nednhi corpses, to hasten their covering, since night burial was a taboo thing in Apache lore. I should have been alerted when the Indian men were so assiduous in what was very hard manual labor, a condition normally abhorrent to the Apache male. But I was deceived by fatigue and anxiety, as well as by my determination that an Apache, being but another child of God, was as other men and, thus, redeemable.

In all of this, neither Allison nor myself was permitted to speak with Little Buck, nor was the boy's headband gag removed so that he might talk aloud. We were likewise refused the simple human charity of touching the lad to reassure him. I essayed a wave in his direction and was promptly smitten across the long bone of my arm with an Apache rifle barrel. Allison, never moving, said out of the side of his mouth to me, "*Cuidado*, Padre, these babies have turnt spooky on us," and I understood the Texas argot plainly enough to obey its injunction entirely. Until the party was ready for the burial, neither Allison nor myself blinked an eyelid except of necessity.

When the digging ceased, Juh informed me that Apache law forbade the presence of *extraños*, aliens, when war dead were being honored. He apologized for the delay but said he knew I realized their law and would remember that Apache dead must be put beneath the ground before the night was flown, or their shades would never stay quiet. Accordingly, the Tejano and myself must now depart with the first part of the band. With us would go Huera, while the white boy would stay with Juh. It might eventuate, he told me, that the ransom would fall through of payment, or other thing go wrong with the scheme of He Who Has The Plan. In that case, Juh had thought seriously to raise the Anglo lad as his own. The boy would make a good Apache and the work of this particular night would be a pertinent beginning for such an adoption. "A good time for first learning," was the way he put it, in finishing.

Naturally, I asked him if he meant to kill the captive scalp hunters when we had gone on. I knew the risk of such intrusions upon Juh's patience, but the question had to be put. Nothing less would be Christian, and Allison, plainly, had lost his Texas tongue.

Or, perhaps, did not want to lose it.

Fortunately, the Nednhi chief remained calm. It was not true, he said, that he or his men would harm the captives. It was simply that they, being the murderers, would now be audience to the last end of the murdered. "They will be held here to witness the presence of death," he said, "to know how it was for other helpless men to die when they could not defend themselves."

I nodded, supposing he referred to the scalper ambush of the Nednhi and, moreover, succumbing to a hard whisper from Allison to, "for God's sake stop augering it; you want to get me and you made witnesses of, too?"

His direct meaning was not clear, but there was an inference to the query I did not care for.

"It is well," I answered Juh. "But how will we carry the woman? A travois will jolt her and start the bleeding again."

"They used her that badly, Blackrobe?"

"As animals. Worse. As human beasts. She is hurt within, Jefe. She cannot bleed more and live."

Ben Allison stepped between us.

Extending his right arm, the palm outward, he spoke earnestly. "Listen to me, *schicho*; I will carry the woman in my arms upon my horse."

Juh moved back, brushing the Texan's hand away.

"We are not friends. The Apache does not answer *schicho* to any *Tejano Diablo*."

I was quick to explain for him that Allison was not a Texas Ranger; that he had but ridden with the ranger band in pursuit of Juh's raiders because he was a friend of the boy's mother; that he had, indeed, promised that poor woman, dying of the lung sickness, to care for the child until he might be returned to his father.

"Is this a true thing, Tejano?" he asked Allison.

"Yes," the Texan said. "Altogether."

Juh stared hard at him. Then nodded. "We are still not brothers," he said. "Pick up the woman."

Allison knelt and gathered Huera to him. At once, two braves came forward with a horse for him. They assisted me in handing up to the Texan, once he was mounted on the animal, Huera's motionless form.

"If she bleeds," Juh said, "so will you bleed."

Ben Allison bobbed his lean head in Indian understanding. Firming his grasp of Huera, he said, in Apache, to his restive pony, "*hoh-shuh*, ride easy," and all was ready.

In that manner—delayed only while Juh dispatched his best scouts, Ka-zanni and Tubac, to follow and report back on the apparent flight toward Casas Grandes of Kifer and the surviving scalpers—we departed Old Campground, going by West Way toward Juh's Stronghold.

The Nednhi named by Juh to remain behind with him and the captive white boy on the fouled beach made no move to bury the Apache dead while our section of the party was yet in sight of Laguna de Luz. I carried away with me a nameless boding of evil to come. Nevertheless, I said nothing to Allison. For his part, the big Texan was occupied with guiding his nervous Indian mount while protecting Huera. Neither did he speak to me. The Apaches, *naturalmente*, ignored us both.

The only voices we heard in the entire labored

climb up out of Old Campground were those of some wolves howling off to the south.

Shivering, I crossed myself.

I did not like the sound; it seemed much nearer than the earlier cry of the solitary *lobo.*

15

At a place in the trail above Old Campground, the Apache halted. Kaytennae, youngest of the group with us, came over to where I held my mount with those of Ben Allison and the rear-guard warrior, a surly fellow whom I did not know. Kaytennae was another matter.

I had known the youth from his twelfth summer, when he had been brought to me near death from what appeared to be a deep brain fever. The good Lord God furnished me the power to heal him and return him to his savage people in health. The Nednhi made Indian payment of the debt. Each summer, after that, the boy had been sent down out of the Sierra to stay at the blackrobe's "school" and be taught the skills of medicine. The Apache, despite all contrary imaginations, were an extremely bright people. The Nednhi well knew that white man and Mexican had many learnings that Indians did not and could not possess, living as they did. In rare cases, as it went against their every barbarian instinct, they would trust a youngster to some priest for tutelage. The priest, of course, understood just as well what the terms of his failure would be.

Kaytennae was a Mexican Apache—most of the hostiles were American bands living in Chihuahua as the occasions of Yanqui pursuit demanded—and a nephew of Juh. He was no more than six-teen in this springtime of the El Paso raid; and he was with the Juh party as "horse boy"—a young Apache soldier's first employment in war. The duty was not a simple one, and its awarding to any young Chiricahua—most warlike of all the Apache peoples—was always of significance. I was certain Kaytennae would be known to a later history, being of the highest intelligence and most supreme wildness.

In the present case, the boy was selected to approach me for the simple reason that none of his fellows seemed disposed to do so. At least, that was my guess.

"Blackrobe," he now said, first touching his forehead to show respect, "look down there."

I did not have to ask where.

We had climbed no more than half a mile. Old Campground lay directly below us, no greater distance downward than perhaps six hundred feet. The moon had risen as we made our way upward and now lit Pool of Light and the white-sanded beach with nearly dazzling brilliance. The eye, unaided, could make out a stone on that pure sand no bigger than the head of a man. Still, I was puzzled at the boy's direction, for the campground lay deserted of visible life. The bodies of the Apache dead had been "honored" and were gone. Gone also were the men and horses with Juh. Plainly, the work of the burial party had been done and that party, with the two scalp hunter prisoners, was on its way up the path by which we had just come to this spectacular overlook.

"What is it, Kaytennae?" I said. "I see nothing down there but some small stones on the beach, one or two, near where the last of the fire smolders."

"Two," the boy said softly.

"Well, yes," I answered. "I see them, if that is what you mean. Is that such a strange thing, *niño*?"

"Not to us," murmured Kaytennae. "Watch."

Allison, listening to the exchange, which was in the bastard Spanish of the *monte*, kneed his horse nearer to us. He had been relieved of Huera's burden by the other Apache, who had the woman resting on a pallet of their blankets while we awaited Juh and the remainder of the party. In consequence we were, for the moment, free of any witness save young Kaytennae. I could sense the Texan's tenseness, as opposed to my own relative calm.

"Can you imagine what the boy is talking about?" I asked him, feeling, in fact, quite relieved and grateful to God to be where we were, alive and with hope to remain that way. The big man nodded quickly.

"I can," he said. Narrowing the pale eyes, he peered hard and for some moments at the distant beach. Then, wiping his eyes, he shook the lean head.

"Damn!" he said, plainly disturbed. "I wish we had them field glasses of Bustamante's."

"Well, they are in the sack of things you left strapped to Mean Trick. Along with my own bag of small belongings similarly fastened to Tin Can. If it has come to wishes, hombre, I could do much better than that. I would say, let the field glasses be here, and let us be there, with dear Lata and sister Jugada. *No es verdad*?"

"Very damn much so," grimaced the Texan.

But there was a surprise here.

Kaytennae, as I had spoken in Spanish, understood the reference.

Reaching into his own war bag, he came forth with a bulky object, which he tendered to me.

"*Gemelos de campaña*," he said. "*Mejicano*."

I accepted the offering, and he spoke the truth; in my hand lay a fine pair of Mexican cavalry field glasses.

Allison took them from me, unbidden.

Almost in the instant that he raised them, granting only a swift moment of focusing, I heard him say, "Oh, Christ," under his breath.

Next moment, Kaytennae had taken the glasses back from him.

"What is it?" I asked the silent Texan.

"It's Custer Johnson and that young feller, Carson."

"The scalpers—they're dead!"

"Worse; alive."

"Thank God!"

"Not hardly," said Ben Allison, low voiced. "They're buried to their necks on the beach."

"*Nombre Dios*! the stones—!"

"Their heads," nodded the Texan. "That's all of them that your friend Juh left sticking out of the sand."

"But why?" I cried out. "For what?"

Into the stillness that fell between us came a sobbing, doleful howling of wolves, immediately near. I felt a chill of ice about my heart. And Allison nodded once more.

"For them," he said.

16

Juh came but half an hour later. We heard the striking of pony hooves upon the trail, then the blowing-out of climbing horses. "Be quiet," Kaytennae warned Allison and me. "Stay in your places." With that he left us to go and await his famed uncle.

When Juh had come up onto the overlook, he went first to the side of Huera. We could hear him speaking to her in Apache, but we could not hear that she replied to him. Presently, he arose and stalked over to where we were. "The woman does not say anything," he said in Spanish to Allison. "What do you say?"

The Texan stood to it quietly.

It was true, he said. Huera had bled on him in the trail up to this place. Easy as he had held her, the motion of the horse beneath them had been exaggerated in the steeper places. The bleeding had begun again. "I will say more, Jefe," he told Juh. "If we do not find a better way to carry her, she is done."

"Jefe," I broke in anxiously, "can we not abide in this place with her long enough to have the blood clot?'

Juh shook his head. The Nednhi chief knew from preliminary scouting that Kifer and five of the scalpers were still at large, and were going toward Casas Grandes which they would reach about the same time as those other Texas Devils who might come to the town following their comrades who had died in the garden of my church. If such a pursuing Tejano force should learn from Kifer of the affair at Old Campground, the trail of the Nednhi to their stronghold would be too fresh for safety. The droppings of the ponies would yet be green. It was a chance of delay that no Apache war leader could accept. Huera, if carrying her would kill her, must then die. They would not leave her for the enemy again.

Both Allison and I understood that this was Indian thinking of the purest sort and not to be denied by any white or Mexican logic. I informed Juh we respected him and would say no more. But I had yet to fully know Ben Allison.

If they must carry the woman, he said to Juh, then there was an Indian way to do it. He, a simple Kwahadi Comanche of the Water Horse band, and so by inheritance from his pureblood grand-mother on his mother's side, need not remind a great leader such as Juh of this way.

Of course not, Juh graciously agreed.

But since the Tejano Comanche brother of the quarter blood had introduced the matter, red courtesy rules required he be permitted the honor of saying the way.

I do not know how Allison kept his face grave, but he did. The way, he said, after thanking Juh for the privilege of saying it, was the old method of two pack animals of utmost reliability being fastened abreast and the Plains Indian blanket-sling being fashioned to stretch between the brutes. It was the easiest known manner of carrying wounded in the field. Even the ignorant White Eye cavalry employed this method with bad cases. Of course, the entire thing was that the two pack animals be of the highest discipline and obedience.

Of course! growled the Nednhi chief.

But did the Tejano see any such animals in this sweat-caked band of wind-broken and hard-run Apache horseflesh? Why, Ysun's name! half of them weren't even Nednhi horses, but stolen settlement mounts barely good enough to carry a single rider in good health.

Was this a sample of Comanche war thinking?

Did Allison's stupidity explain, perhaps, the fact of the great Tsaoh people's growing weakness in war?

Tsaoh was a borrowed Comanche word of uncertain other origin meaning approximately "enemy." It was one of their own names for themselves, and Ben understood it.

He would never, the Texan apologized, dare to suggest a thing without having its full details in his mind; he would expect anger from that. But, in the present case, he had the two pack animals not only in his mind but to his immediate hand. Juh had but to grant him two warriors, or go with him himself, and he, Allison, would lead them directly to the best double-sling carriers in the Indian country.

With this boast, he muttered aside to me that he hoped devoutly that Tin Can and Mean Trick would live up to his recommendation. For, he added, if they did not, neither would we. *Live,* he explained gratuitously.

I had no time to reply to him.

Juh told the others to wait for him. He then called young Kaytennae to his side and said, "Get your horse." Thus it was that Ben Allison rode back with Juh, warchief of all the Nednhi, and his acolyte nephew Kaytennae, to bring up the hinny twins. But a terrible and ugly thing came first to pass.

When Kaytennae had found his mount, and Ben Allison regained his, Juh raised a hand and grunted, "Wait."

With the command, he went afoot to the edge of the overlook. I went with him on an instinct of fear.

Pointing below, he said to me as matter-of-factly as if the delay were merely one of camp-breaking detail, "We must wait, you see, Blackrobe, until our brothers have dined. Should we return at this time, we would frighten them off. They are extremely timid, you know."

There was a pause, during which I heard the crunch of pebbles beneath *n'deh b'keh* behind me, and I sensed, rather than saw, the tall form of the Texan move up to join us. In my continuing, incomprehensible innocence, I still did not realize what the Nednhi was saying.

Allison did, *por supuesto.*

"Padre," he said, in his soft San Saba drawl,

"you'd best go tend the woman. This ain't your game."

Then I knew. Then I turned to go, queasy of the gut already, but grateful. But I was too slow by half a turn. In the corner of my eye, I saw the first of the crouching shadows melt out of the south rocks of Old Campground. I waited, even then, to be sure, and, in the silence on the mountainside, I heard distinctly their first excited whimperings and the horrid chopping of the jawteeth induced by the sighting and smelling of the bloodied baits before them.

I fled then to the side of Huera.

Hooding my cowl, I prayed to hear no more.

But I did hear.

I hear that frightful sound yet.

It was not alone the slavering and bickering of the wolves among themselves, but the human cries of impossible agony that preceded the end. Pray God I shall never see purgatory. But I have already heard it.

It was when the wolves came for the heads of Custer Johnson and the youth, Billy Jo Carson, at Old Campground of the Chiricahua.

And ate them, to the sand of the beach, alive.

17

The hinny mules behaved as though broken to the work of the in-between sling. Moreover, West Way, as far as the Cañon Avariento, proved not a difficult track. It was neither as steep nor as dangerously narrow as the trail into Old Campground from Casas Grandes. Remarking on this welcome surprise, I was cautioned by Allison to "wait up a bit."

"Happen I know Injuns," he nodded. "We'll come to where she squeezes down like a tight-choked side-by-each."

"Like a what, hombre?"

"A double-barreled scatter-gun bored full-and-full."

"Ah!"

I naturally had no precise idea what he was talking about.

But, as usual, I got what he called "the drift" of his aromatic Texas speech. Perhaps, in this case, it was only because the word *avariento* had the meaning of "narrow," among several others permitting one to surmise that Cañon Avariento might prove to be well named. The Indians seldom erred in these appellations.

We rode the night away with only two halts to tighten saddles and to see to Huera's condition. It was nearing dawn when Juh called the third halt.

At this point the Apache horses had been on the force for twenty hours. They were ridden down to their hocks and at least half of them would be fit only for wolf baiting, hereafter. The remaining half would recover with rest, but could not carry their riders an added mile, presently, even if beaten to it. They were simply done.

Juh came to me, his shadow Kaytennae by his side.

"Blackrobe," he said, "your small mules appear yet sound. I want you to go by their heads, however, from this place. The way will be difficult and I am sure they will travel it better if following you. Kaytennae will be your guide, in turn. Tejano," he said to Allison, "come with me."

"*Anh*, Jefe," the Texan answered quickly. "You bet." Then, quietly aside to me, in leaving, "Padre, if this here is where we split the blanket, good luck with your half. You ain't very big, but you will do for full-groomed."

"*Hasta lo vista*," I said, and they were gone.

"Well," Kaytennae said cheerfully, "come on, Blackrobe. Let us see if we can bring my aunt safely to the next place. *Ugashe*."

"Your aunt?" I asked, following him. "I thought she was Juh's aunt."

"She is, of course."

"By blood, *niño*?"

"Well, no."

"Ah. Neither is she to you, I suspect."

"No, not by blood."

To the Apache, the term aunt is like that of brother or cousin. In most usages no blood kinship exists by employment of the word. If the person is a real cousin, for example, the Nednhi will say that he is "son to the sister of my own-mother." Apaches, among themselves, can distinguish the matter simply by the inflection with which they say aunt or brother or cousin. Occasionally, usually with outsiders, they qualify it by saying own-brother or own-cousin, the "own" meaning a real or true kinsman by blood. Exactly the same applies to grandparents, sons, daughters, any relationship at all. A strange people, as previously held.

For the moment, I felt relieved that Huera was not, in fact, kin to Juh's dark bloodline. The Nednhi headman was a fine specimen of his wild kind, but so purely an Apache, a *bárbaro* committed to hating the white man, that I did not wish to think of graceful Huera being of his same family. For I had to remember that the Apache always hates another man even before he hates the white man, and that is the Mexican man, of course. And I, Alvar Nunez, allowing for my inclusion of Opata blood, was a Mexican man.

Thus cautioned, I went gladly with young Kaytennae to the side of the fitfully sleeping warrior woman. And thus, with the youth before me in the stygian gloom of the predawn, I went with my silent Huera and the two small mules into what Apache fate I knew not. Nor, God forgive me, did I care, so long as I might share it with her.

Now the trail went upward. Now it narrowed as Allison had predicted. Even young Kaytennae panted with the climbing. No other two Spanish mules could have borne that blanket-sling with precious Huera in it as dear Lata and Jugada bore it. So careful in each choice of step. So strong and steady in every upward heave of wither and hindquarter. Not one slip, in all the miles of the desperate going, for either little brute's burro-trim hooves. They went like trained dogs, watching their burden constantly, never squeezing the woman, never bumping her. All of this with the moon long set and the way lighted only by the blackness that inks that canyoned land at the deepest hour of the night, just before the new day.

Sunrise found us in a pass which showed nothing but ranges before us and behind us.

I was certain we were on the divide and that this would be the place of the fourth halt. It was not.

Down we went now.

The way eased somewhat, the bare granite gave way to a beginning of meadowed softlands. Pine and spruce and balsam fir foresting set in and, before long, we were in a lovely timbered country. Within a mile, we heard fast-falling water and shortly we came out upon a small but furious stream rushing to the west; we had crossed to the other drainage and were on the Pacific Slope of the Sierra.

Kaytennae confirmed the fact but said we must keep up with the others, now nearly out of sight ahead of us. I noted that, even afoot, the pace of the march did not seem to yield. Again, the youth agreed, pointing out as a true thing the story I had so often heard that a healthy Apache of young or middle years will indeed keep up with a horse and, in fact, over a distance, outtravel the animal. "Before the horse came here," the youth now told me, "the Apache ran everywhere that he went. He never just walked as a white man or Mexican will. He trotted as the *lobo*, even loped as the *caballo*. We can still do it, as you see. We warriors can."

"Very well, warrior," I answered him back, "I am not so certain we priests can compete with the wolf and the horse, but these Spanish mules will try. *Vamos*! *a ello*!"

For the next six hours, until high noon, we slid and groped and fought and prayed our way down out of the Blue Mountains of the Nednhi, coming at last and with God's goodness to the "fourth place," where Juh and the others stood awaiting us.

But God and His goodness were fleeting.

The fourth place proved no more final than the first or third halting; we rested, boiled a little of Bustamante's tea, watered the twin mules, examined and performed what care we might upon Huera, and pushed on.

We were down in the foothills of the west side now, following a course southward whichcrossed the mouths of the innumerable barrancas that ran back into the high country. These openings offered a continuing opportunity of advantage to the Apache march, Kaytennae explained.

First, there was the matter of hand-close concealment in the deep fissures. Then, many of them bore local water courses, which made for rich backlands where small game, good pasturage, and, indeed, some farming of the ancients still were to be found. At one place, we followed one of the streams a considerable distance inland. There we found delicious fruits growing along the banks, evidences of old irrigations by *Indios reducidos*, enslaved or tamed Indians, of another time. The waters also teemed with game fish. Yet when I suggested to Kaytennae that Huera's strength would be well restored by a good meal of trout boiled down into a fish gruel, the Nednhi youth recoiled.

"Blackrobe," he admonished me, "you should know better than to say that thing. An Apache cannot eat the flesh of the fish, no more than that of the dog. But I will not report it to my uncle. Be warned."

"I would not blame you, if you told him, *niño*,"

I said guiltily, and I promised to take future care.

"But your aunt must eat," I added. "Perhaps this one time—"

"*Chito, chito*!" he cried, "hush at once."

We went on, trailing behind the Apaches who now followed Juh and Ben Allison back into the hills. The canyon we were in widened abruptly. Before us was a deserted settlement, the adobes washed away, roof timbers dry-rotted into caving tumbles. Inside one foundation square grew a pine tree no less than thirty feet high. Beyond the ruined hutments ran a tangle of ancient orange trees which, miracle of miracles, yet bore a tasty fruit. We also noted palms growing here which had been planted by the hand of man. Kaytennae grew uneasy going through this musty place of the past. He said he did not understand how white men and Mexicans could bear to stay in such airless dwellings. For him, they would be as traps that had caught him. "How can your people live in this manner?" he asked me. "How do they see the stars at night? Or taste the clean bite of the air?"

Juh and the others shared the young man's restlessness. We should have halted there but did not. I had only time to gather my cowl full of the sweet oranges for Huera's eating, and we were traveling again.

But now we were coming to it.

Suddenly, we were into a flare of the higher canyon floor. Vertical walls of rock went straight up, hundreds of feet above us. Upon the south wall was a black split, you could call it nothing better, really. Just a place where the mother rock had cracked open far enough and high enough to admit one man on horseback, or two men on foot walking abreast but very closely.

Kaytennae saw my look of dismay, and he grinned happily.

"Cañon Avariento," he said.

I could not credit his words. *That* was a canyon? That miserable schism in the granite's great cliff was famed Cañon Avariento? The legendary *entrada* to Juh's Stronghold? Kaytennae joked with me.

"*Niño*," I said, "*por favor, no hace chacota*."

"But I do not make fun, Blackrobe."

"No? God's Name! We will go into that hole?"

"*Anh*," he nodded eagerly. "Right now."

So we did, too, I carrying Huera in my own arms while Kaytennae passed the hinny mules one at a time through the vile varmint's cavern beckoning ahead. We went on blindly through the rock, feeling its walls with our hands to avoid striking head or toe or tender shin on the ever-intruding stone fangs of its riven jaws. I actually crept through backward, thus to avoid accidentally injuring the poor creature in my charge. So it was that, when we came again into daylight, breaking free of the mountain, I stood at first with my rear to the vista that, upon turning myself to the fore, smote the eye so astoundingly as to bring from me an awed, *"Father, Son, and Holy Spirit—!"*

The whole interior range of the Sierra appeared to open before us.

We stood in a rocky amphitheater, black with the campfire smoke of Apache centuries. From it, the view inward of the range, framed a distant, towering mesa crowned with a thin green line of timber. The incredible bulk of this apparent monolith staggered the mind. It seemed like there was a separate world awaiting us up there on the top. One sensed it. One understood that. Without a word from young Kaytennae, I knew we were going up there. And I knew what awaited us on the mesa.

Kaytennae saw that my imagination had guessed it.

"*Anh*, yes, Blackrobe," he said. "Our home."

I could only nod mutely for reply.

I was looking on a sight never before seen by Anglo or Mexican traveler living to describe it.

I was looking at Juh's Stronghold.

18

Shortly, Juh came over to us and spoke to Kaytennae in Apache. At once, the youth took from his war bag a common small mirror of the variety carried by both Mexican and American cavalry troops in the field. Although it was not specifically a heliographic mirror, I was quickly interested to see it so used now. My interest stemmed in direct part from the fact that Kaytennae had learned this playful art from a certain priest in Casas Grandes. I had provided him the glass to while away his convalescence from the brain fever. I had subsequently learned from Juh that the lad could send and receive the sun-flashes of such signaling better than any adult in the band.

Now we stood by while Kaytennae sent his blinding flashes up to the mesa's top. They were answered before long, and the youth told Juh that the return flashings promised that fresh horses would be started down at once, as well as medicine.

"*Un-nuh*," grunted the chief. "Meanwhile we will wait."

Unbidden, we all sought our places to sit down. A fire was built and water put to boil. I made Huera as comfortable as possible. Allison came over to wait with us, but Little Buck remained at Juh's side. The Texan told me that, in the entire night of riding and walking, the Apaches had not permitted one word between himself and the boy. It was, he believed, the beginning of the white captive's training into Apachehood. He was to know that his people were forever behind him, that he was no longer Pinda Lickoyi, a White

Eye, but Tindé, of the Apache themselves. "We give them another week or ten days with the kid," he concluded, "he won't want to talk to us if they let him."

"No, no, not so swiftly as that," I denied. "But he will change."

"You don't need to draw me no pictures, Padre," he nodded. "I've seen the Comanche break a white kid."

We fell still, for Juh was scowling over at us.

It was midafternoon now. The hours wore on. Huera became restless beneath the crawl of deer flies and the heat of the late day. She became first pale, then flushed. The Texan and I touched her skin, exchanged frowns. It was what we had feared. The fever.

Allison leaned deeply over her, sniffing like some lean hound on track. He looked up at me, grimacing.

"I can smell it," he said. "She's festered."

I leaned and sniffed in turn, shook my head.

"I do not detect it, hombre."

"That's because you ain't smelt enough of it, Padre; I got four years of its stink in my nose: three in the war, one on the owlhoot trail. She's festered. We don't do something *más pronto*, she'll go to gangrene, *inside*."

"God forbid!"

"Mebbe," he rasped. "But we better dicker with Juh."

He went over to the Nednhi chief before I could move to dissuade him. I could only follow quickly, in hope of apologizing for his rude bluntness and lack of courtesy rules. In this entire situation, I understood something that Allison did not appear to grasp. It was that my own life was at least somewhat respected by the wild mountain tribesmen; while his life lay continually as near its end as one rise of anger in Juh's savage temper, or one improper challenge of Juh's supremacy. I had tried impressing this upon the Texan in the very outset of our adventure, away back at the Nednhi Falls. He had shrugged it off by reminding me that Juh was my department. He was on the trail to get back Little Buck Buckles and I was along solely to pacify the Apache in the process of the rescue.

I suspected I would get the same answer now, but the opportunity to learn so was denied.

Juh was already rumbling with rage.

He was, in fact, picking up his beautiful new Winchester rifle and working its yellow brass lever to emplace a cartridge in the loading chamber.

Ben Allison was the cock of that rifle's hammer from his death.

He moved faster than Juh's finger on the trigger.

Knocking the rifle barrel upward with a kick of his foot, Allison turned and bent down with his back into the weapon and the burly Nednhi chieftain. Both of the Texan's sinewy hands seized the barrel in the same instant that Juh's finger closed and the heavy blast of the explosion of the round-in-chamber echoed off up-canyon. With all the force in his lean body, the Texan heaved on the rifle barrel. As Juh did not let go of the weapon's stock, he perforce followed the arc of its swing over the Texan's back. Juh landed on the rocks of the floor of the halting place, flat on his broad back. The grunt of the air driven from his great lungs by the impact was of explosive force. For a moment he lay stunned. Then, he was on his feet, finding Ben Allison with his eyes.

"Tejano, you are a dead man," he croaked hoarsely. "Give me the rifle."

"I will give it to you, where you were going to give it to me," Allison answered him, working the loading lever. "Right in your damned *intestinos. Entiende*, Jefe?"

Juh, for all his Apache fury, did comprehend.

His warriors had all closed in a tight circle about the big Texan, but they could not fire into him without danger of the same bullets striking their chief. Allison, however, had a clear field of fire and a range of not over four feet. Under those circumstances not even the warchief of all the Nednhis wanted to get shot in the guts. The Apache, moreover, was the supreme realist. It was a trait of his people. An Apache will always seek to live. Always.

"You have the rifle, Tejano," he said. "Use it, or say what else you will say to me."

"Sure enough," Ben Allison said, pale eyes never leaving the dark ones glaring at him. "This time, try listening, Jefe. I won't miss like you did."

It was here that I came out from behind the rock where I had sought refuge, ears yet ringing from the rifle's discharge.

"*Por favor,*" I pleaded with Juh, "let me speak for this *tonto.* I know what he was trying to say to you, Jefe. He does not understand that the Apache do not use the hand-sign language. Remember always that he carries the Comanche blood. They are children of the plains. They talk with their hands. But this *hombre alto* was speaking from his heart, Jefe. Believe it. May I speak now? A life very dear to you depends upon it."

"*Uh-nuh,*" Juh nodded and looked away from Ben Allison. For his part, the Texan retained the Winchester and kept it also on the cock, its gaping .44-caliber bore trained on the belly of Juh. The Nednhi could feel it there, without looking. So could I. It was a trying moment for us all.

But Huera's rising fever brought her to cry out in wordless confusion of mind, and it was like the cry of a wounded animal in a trap, dying, or knowing it was about to die. That sound broke even the granite of Juh's terrible face.

"Go on, *jorobado,*" he said. "Speak."

Rapidly, I told him that the Texan had determined that Huera's interior woundings, from the rape of the scalp hunters, had become dangerously infected. He could determine this by scent, where I, an experienced doctor, could not yet detect such odor. The woman must receive treatment immediately. If she did not, the rotting disease, as the Nednhi called gangrenous morbid tissues of the body, would swiftly claim her. Allison, I urged, knew of such treatment.

This was no falsehood of desperation, I explained to the glaring warchief. The Tejano had only now told me that, back in the ruins of the orange trees, he had noted growth of a particular weed plant familiar to him from the Comanche country. If not precisely the plant, then it was of the same family and, hopefully, of near enough kinship to hold similar medicinal values. It was this sudden remembering that had brought the tall stranger to accost Juh so bluntly the moment before.

"Allison seeks only your permission to go now, at once, and return with the flowers of this plant which hold magical power to cure the fester of inner wounds." I sparred with the angry Juh. "Will you say yes, Jefe?"

He would not look at me yet.

I thought, even then, he would refuse. A warrior of his reputation who has been humbled before his fighting men has received his own grievous inner wounds. Again, it was a soft moaning from Huera that decided him. Or, rather, stirred him to continue.

"*Un-nuh*," he nodded. "Let Allison describe the blossoms. I will send Kaytennae back for some of them."

I turned to the Texan with this offer, but he promptly shook his head. "Jefe," he said, in Spanish, to the Nednhi, "suppose the boy picked some of the other flowers back there, which grow by those we need, and which are so nearly the same as to defy separation except by a medicine healer."

Juh looked at Ben Allison.

"*You* are a medicine healer?" he challenged.

"My Kwahadi grandmother, who was an own-sister to Pete Nocono, father of Quanah Parker, was a healer. I learned from her."

"I think you lie to save your life."

"I do not, Jefe; I tell the truth to save another's life. Think of this: can you not always kill me after the woman lives?"

Juh had to admit the Apache logic of this thought. One imagined to see, even, a hint of grudging admiration in the scowling nod.

His answer, however, failed to echo any such softening. "I have already said that you are a dead man," he now told Allison, "but I want the woman to live." He paused, the scowl darkening. "The question is only of that matter. And I do not trust you or this humpbacked priest of Casas Grandes. We will wait for our own medicines. You heard Kaytennae say the people were sending these down the Zig Zag Trail with the fresh horses."

Allison glanced at me, and I could not help him.

In the silence, young Kaytennae spoke.

"*Anh*, yes!" he said, excitedly. "Look up there on the great cliff of the trail. There, about a third of the way down. You see where that long blaze of white-colored rock is? Do you note the dark line of the trail crossing its face? *Anh*, of course. Watch now and you will see the people, with the horses, crawling over that great light-colored rock."

The stillness deepened as we squinted upward where the late sun painted the west wall of the monolith mesa.

I could see nothing at first. Then, of a sudden, I did see Kaytennae's small "dark line." It was not as of horses and men, however, but of the tiniest antlike specks. In the pellucid mountain light, the distance to the mesa deceived even the eyes of an *hombre del monte* such as myself. I was momentarily overwhelmed by the magnitude, the mystique, of Juh's fearful stonghold.

Not so Ben Allison.

"The people are one hour down that trail," he said, speaking to Kaytennae, "and two hours yet from the bottom of it. *No es verdad*, hombre?"

It was a skilled thing to call the youngster a man; Kaytennae stood a visible bit taller for the courtesy.

"Yes, that is true," he said. "They will be here with the sunset."

"Just so," Allison nodded. "With the sunset, also, the woman will be already dying."

I was watching Juh when he said this, and I thought to see the warchief's bronze face show emotion.

Juh, let me explain, was different from the other Chiricahua. He had neither the fine features and light color of the Warm Springs band, the chiseled profile and leaner physique of the Cochise band, nor the short, flat-boned, almost Comanchean look common to the Bedonkohes. He had been described in that time, by Anglos who knew him, as appearing more Asiatic than Apache. One American officer, an erstwhile reservation agent, who had met Juh more often than any other white man had, said that the Nednhi chief was a reincarnation of the Mongol barbarian of four centuries gone, "Mongoloid in form, feature, every aspect of the Tamerlanian horseman."

Now, looking at Juh, as he stared at the Texan, I understood for the first time this peculiar difference.

He did seem a stranger among his own kind.

"Tejano," he said, almost gently, "what are the flowers called?"

"The butterfly weed," Allison answered. "It is an orange prairie milkweed."

"How does it work?"

The Texan had explained the medicinal effect to me so that I understood it to be a powerful diaphoretic and expectorant. That is to say, it would cause profuse sweating and induce coughing up of excess body fluids, cleaning the system as a purgative. I now put these qualities into Apache terms for Juh, seeing that Allison was beyond his depth in doing so.

When I had done, the Nednhi merely nodded.

"Bring up the Tejano boy," he ordered his men.

Little Buck was dragged forward and Juh put his hand on the lad's head. "If you are not returned within the hour," he told Ben Allison, "this small head will be carried up the Zig Zag Trail in a sack."

I saw the Texan's pale eyes turn cold.

I did not believe Juh would behead the boy, for we were now brief hours from the meeting with He Who Has The Plan and the possible fruition of the ransom plot.

Yet Juh, Mongol atavism or not, was an Apache.

Neither He Who Has The Plan, Ben Allison of San Saba, nor Father Panfilo Alvar Nunez of Casas Grandes could stay his dark hand should that hand be seized with the madness of *hesh-ke*, the unreasoning Apache rage to kill.

The difference was that Ben Allison had played

this game before, and he knew its deadly rules.

In a snaking lunge too swift to follow, the Texan seized Kaytennae and whirled him into helpless lock of one long arm. The youth's body was held between Allison's own and the Apache pack that was backing Juh. The muzzle of the short Winchester rifle was jammed beneath the boy's ear.

"*Ojo por ojo*," he told Juh. "If I return to find the white boy's head held in a sack, you will find this Apache cub's brains blown out upon your canyon wall, believe it. Do we have an understanding?"

I thought to see Juh's eyeballs burst from his skull. But he loved Kaytennae.

"*Lo entiendo*," he grated.

"*Basta*," rasped Ben Allison and turned and went with Kaytennae back into the riven cliff.

19

Allison and Kaytennae were returned with the flowers of the butterfly weed within the hour. Meanwhile, the condition of Huera had worsened. The Nednhi had gathered about her fetid pallet and were muttering that they could smell the odor of the rotting death. Allison, sniffing the same air, confided to me that he thought otherwise but that we must let the Apaches continue to believe their holy woman lay dying. In that way, if his Comanche potion broke the fatal fever, the Nednhi would think we had greater power than Huera, thereby improving our own chances of survival.

Agreeing, I bid the Texan recall that Huera had proclaimed him a devil, a vanished spirit from the pile of ranger bodies in the mission garden. If he succeeded now in saving her, the Apaches would also be more inclined to accept his seeming return to human form, a matter that surely had been worrying them. “A witch doctor or medicine healer is quite another thing from an evil spirit,” I advised him. “Do your best.”

Allison said nothing to this, but fell instead to his perilous work.

There is little use to detail it; it would be credible only to the barbarian mind: within the following hour and by use of the boiled extract of the weed blooms, the Texan had induced a sweat in the woman such as I had never seen—she exuded a veritable torrent of vile fluids-of-evil from her pores—and not alone was the deep fever broken, but the woman was sitting up, clear-eyed, asking for food to eat.

The Nednhi, Juh among them, went quickly and quietly to their saddlebags and brought forth mule jerky, dried fruits of the prickly-pear cactus, and earth-baked mescal root. All watched in rapt silence as the war chief himself fed the recovering holy woman.

Allison and I heaved a joint sigh. For added personal emphasis to our gratitude, I made a *cruz* in the air. Seeing it, the Texan nodded, "Make mine the same, Padre," he said, and did not smile, saying it. As soberly, I made a second *cruz* for him.

You may believe we were not laughing. When I have said Ben Allison was a man of outrageous native humor, it is not the same, at all, as saying that he was himself an odd or lumpish fellow. Entirely to the contrary. Standing there in that chancefully gained moment of relief, the wheaten mane of crudely barbered hair, the restless wolflike eyes, the bony, muscular tallness of him, the Comanche-dark complexion, all conspired to render of the Texan the most compelling picture of a frontier *pistolero más peligroso.* Yet it was the remarkable measure of the man that, in the same silent pause wherein I gauged the dangerous and romantic look of him, he would humbly ask a Catholic blessing.

As though they, too, respected the sign, the Apaches now let us alone, busying themselves with cleaning the captured new Winchester rifles, eating, and smoking. Their talk was of the Texas raid, but guarded, and we caught nothing of value in it. Presently, most of them slept. We ourselves drowsed; the day faded.

The Apaches from the mesa came in at sundown.

There was a greeting flurry but, as the ascent of the great cliff could not be risked by dark, we prepared to spend the night there in Waiting Camp of Cañon Avariento. It was a practice of the centuries for the Indians. Here they would rest after descending the cliff or, if returning from war or trading journey, before reclimbing it. As well, it served as a traditional meeting ground for those other Chiricahuan bands that might come this far to visit Juh's remote people, but not care to scale the great mesa wall itself.

Such jots and tittles of information were cheerfully furnished Allison and myself by young Kaytennae.

The youth had been assigned by Juh to "join our fire," presumably to watch us as we watched Huera. Kaytennae was a delightful companion. He understood considerable English from his days with me in Casas Grandes. He also spoke enough of it to make himself clear when need be. That he kept his ability to himself only showed the keenness of his mind; not even his fierce uncle knew that the youth had learned the *inglés*, at *Misión de la Virgen de Guadalupe*. Yet, curiously, Kaytennae now chose to share his secret, unasked, with an entire stranger. The confidence was a tribute to the Texan. Rare men are like that. You easily tell them things you would not confess to your bishop. Children impose trusts upon them. Women cluck over them. Lost dogs follow them home. And acolyte Apache warriors are brought to give them aid and comfort, even if they are the enemy.

Kaytennae imparted truths to us that night, at his own offer, which could not have been drawn from him under torture. He began by telling Ben Allison that he was not born into the Nednhi band, but adopted by it, utter news to me. He was, moreover, unknown as to precise years, having come to the Nednhi only a short time before those people brought him to me. Indeed, he had been found wandering alone, in the same high fever that I had treated, which by its nature left his memory clouded upon recovery.

By feature and physique, handsome of the one, graceful of the other, the Nednhi thought him to have come from the Warm Springs people, a Chiricahuan family living near Ojo Caliente, in the New Mexico country. But those people, under their hard-fighting leaders, Nana and Victorio, were so warlike and rebellious as to be continually on the run from the American horse soldiers, and so it became increasingly difficult to contact them. Kaytennae had settled in with the Nednhi and become a Mexican Apache of record. Indeed, he now informed us proudly, Juh planned the new name ceremony for him upon return to the mesa. This because of the high quality of his conduct in the El Paso raid, a notably dangerous mission.

"I will be called Looking Glass," he told us.

"This from my ableness to signal with the sun-mirror."

We congratulated him, asking if he preferred to have that name used. He was at once apprehensive, saying that to employ the new name before the ceremony would be worse than for a warrior to look upon the face of his mother-in-law previous to a war party departure. So he remained Kaytennae to us then, and to myself so long as I knew him.

At the very last of our low-voiced talk that warm spring night in Cañon Avariento, the Apache youth looked carefully to see that his elders were all intent about their own, larger fire—where a deer carcass was being spit-roasted and the mescal *bota* passed freely—then turned back to us frowning seriously.

A great trouble had come among his people, he said.

It was something he must tell us.

Kaytennae did not want Allison, who had saved the life of his aunt Huera, and who had shown the courage of a Spanish bull under the angry rifle of Juh, to go up on the mesa unwarned.

Por supuesto, he added, sensing my hurt, his dear teacher Blackrobe Jorobado was an equal worry to his heart. Still, the greater peril awaited the big Tejano. It was for him that death lurked up there in the meadowed forests of Juh's Stronghold. The respectful truce that Juh had extended to the Texan, was an Apache grace entirely.

And the one who awaited Allison and myself up on the mesa was *not* an Apache.

"What is that you say, *niño*?" I interrupted quickly. "Not an Apache? Aha! We had suspected as much. Are you now telling us that He Who Has The Plan is indeed an *extraño*, an alien?"

"Completely, Blackrobe."

"Very interesting, *hijo*. But if he is not of our land, then of which land? And what race?"

"*Chitón*!" said the youth softly. "Juh comes."

Allison and I looked up across the fire. Juh towered there, broad Mongol face staring down at us.

"*Párese*," he ordered Kaytennae, "stand up."

The boy did so and Juh scowled heavily and fingered the coil of his pony quirt as though he weighed a decision to strike the youth across the mouth with its braided horsehide lash.

Yet to hit another in the face is the severest of Apache insults, warranting a return of violence, even of murder. Hence, although he had been drinking steadily with his fellows, Juh let fall to his side the hand that gripped the quirt. The coil loosened, hung slack.

"*Ugashe*," he rumbled, "go."

Kaytennae departed, not looking back.

"Blackrobe," Juh said, deep voice slurred with mescal, "you know I do not want you bothering that boy. He is a talker and you have an advantage over him, besides. Why do you harry me?"

"Jefe," I assured him, "we exchanged nothing but talk of the trail."

"That is a lie. I heard the name of He Who Has The Plan."

"It may be true, Jefe. If so, it came about in a natural way of discussing the journey. Was the boy forbidden to hear that name, or to speak it?"

"No."

"Do you yourself care to tell us of this man? To let us hear his name? Kaytennae refused; absolutely."

"*Enjuh*, I am glad I did not cut him with the *látigo*."

"We are all glad, Jefe. *Un-nuh*."

"*Un-nuh*," he echoed and seemed settled of mind.

But Allison held up a long Texas arm.

"*Momento*, Jefe. Will you tell us of the boy, Little Buck? I would not mention it except that I promised his mother to look after him. You know of that."

At first halting glower, Juh appeared angered by this broaching of a forbidden subject. Yet the Apache's love of children is overriding, and the Nednhi, for all his murderous reputation, was reached. He stepped back to our fire, the change in his demeanor marked.

"That *ish-ke-ne*, that boy-child, he manners

himself like no other whelp of the Pinda Lickoyi that I have ever caught. He fears nothing. He does what he is told. He rides as if your Comanche people had taught him. He eats raw mule. His Spanish is better than your Spanish. He has his own war song, which he sings in a fine, clear voice and has promised to teach me its tune and wordings. His body is *muy duro* for a white boy, and inside he is like us; what must be done, he does; nor has he wept one tear for his mother, or his father, or for anything of his old life. *Wagh*—!"

Wagh being the universal expression of "well done" among horseback Indians, particularly where a show of fortitude has been made, we understood that Little Buck had just been importantly honored.

"*Wagh*, Jefe!" I enthused, waving him adieu. "*Mil gracias. Buenas noches. Buenos sueños.*"

"*Hasta luego*," Allison added.

Juh did not answer. The Texan and I stood and watched him weave his unsteady way back to the mescal and half-burned deermeat. When we sat down again by our dying guard-fire, Allison suggested we "tote up" our blessings. It proved very short work.

For the moment, our health prospered with that of our patient. As a sometime benefactor of these wild people, I myself might survive a failure in Huera's recovery. Allison would not. In the

Apache mind he was now responsible for the warrior woman's life. If that life faltered, so did his. And if it failed altogether, he at once reverted to being merely the seventh of the hated Texas Devils, the only one who had escaped their Apache vengeance in the garden of the hump-backed priest, at Casas Grandes. Moreover, even if the woman recovered, she could, with the whim of any next moment, decide that the big Tejano was still an evil shade and must so be exorcised.

In all of this, there remained one grim certainty.

Tomorrow would take us to the mesa's top and to our meeting with the alien stranger who had gained control of these fiercest of Chiricahuan peoples. The prospect, insofar as we had deliberately aborted the very life of his plan—delivery of the ransom note—brought a minimum of sleep to Allison and I through that very long, dark night at Waiting Camp, in Cañon Avariento, below Juh's Stronghold.

20

The great cliff of the Zig Zag Trail was like that of the Nednhi drop-off in the canyon of the Rio Casas Grandes, only thrice its height. In the four-hour climb I did not see Ben Allison or Little Buck, as the interminable hairpinnings of the track prevented the tail of our line from seeing its head. But I knew they were in the van with Juh and so as safe as any mortals might be in scaling such a fearsome place. As for my charge, Huera, all went well. The Apaches had fashioned a tandem sling in place of the abreast model, so that the warrior woman was carried behind one of the hinnies and before the other. This permitted Tin Can to set the pace and Mean Trick to shoulder the greater weight. It was precarious around some of the switchback turns but, on the worst of them, the Nednhi men came back and unhitched the rear mule, guiding the sling past the bad place by man power. In this manner, well before noon, we came out at the top into a U-notch defile which Kaytennae, traveling with me the entire way, said would lead us directly into Juh's rancheria. Even so prepared, I was not ready for what followed.

We did not go one hundred *pasos* through that square cut in the living rock before we broke into the open.

I literally gasped at the view.

There it was, the fabled stronghold of the Nednhi Apache. All spread before me and so beautiful as to be unreal. It was more a dream than a thing of actual earth and stone and grass and timbered woodland. Lying as it did, immediately back from the great cliff, but hidden by the bastion of the cliff's crest, it was planned by the Creator both as a haven and a heaven for his Apache children. A perfect saucer, half a mile in diameter, its gently sloping outer flange met the pine forests on three sides away from the west wall and these virgin stands of conifer ran until the eye lost them with distance. Yet the vicinity of the camp itself was a meadow of thickest mountain grasses, and Kaytennae told me similar grazing breaks in the timber dotted the entire mesa. He did not know the extent of the mesa's table in its whole, but he said it required a pleasant two-day ride to circle it and that, in all that way, no other trail of ingress or egress passable to horse and rider broke the great rock's scarp.

A clear mountain stream flowed loopingly through the principal meadow of the encampment, watering the permanent beehive jacals and more temporary brush wickiups and ramadas that dis-tinguish every Apache settlement, and furnishing even some limited irrigation to the several small cornfields and bean and melon patches which so surprised me at this altitude.

The stream, at the moment of our exit from the defile, was full of laughing and yelling Apache children and rimmed by women bent to the family laundering stones; standing idly in the water were dozens of the graceful Indian ponies of the Nednhi herd that was on loose graze to forest's edge. In the "town square" of the rancheria, which as in all Indian encampments was circular, old men tossed smooth creekstones at lines drawn in the warm dust, and everywhere in the quiet sunlight of the morning hung the smoke haze and wondrous smells of pitch-pine breakfast fires.

At my side, young Kaytennae nodded and said, "*Estamos en casa,* we are at home."

"*Qué bonito*, *qué belleza*," I said. "It does not seem that any evil could dwell here."

"*Cuidado*," the slender warrior warned. "Here is Juh again, coming to take Huera from us." The party was spreading out to take different pathways into the rancheria, causing the warchief some delay as he bid now this and now the other member of the successful El Paso raid a sober *gracias* for their part. Kaytennae lowered his voice, scarcely moved his lips. "Be very careful with all that you say and do up here, Blackrobe," he muttered. "Remember that He Who Has The Plan is not of your faith. Particularly, you must not depend on us to help you. The people have listened to this *extraño.* He has them all in his hand like you have the Mexicans down in Casas Grandes. In no case must you believe your robes or your *cruz* will prevail as they have before. That is all I can say."

There remained a moment yet before Juh was up to us, and I spent it saying good-bye to Huera. She still lay in the sling, with Lata fore and Jugada aft. As I touched her forehead with my fingers, she opened her eyes, not yet knowing where she had come. "You are come home again," I told her. "We have brought you up the Zig Zag Trail. The big Tejano treated you for your hurts. Do you remember?"

She frowned, as though in useless effort to recall, then shook her head. "No, Blackrobe. Where was that?"

I did not wish to remind her of the terror at Old Campground, and so I said, "Do not concern yourself, Huera. Do you remember me?"

"*Anh,* yes; we were going to take the letter to *el gobernador*, you and I. But something happened—"

"Yes," I said. Again, I did not care to recall to her memory the missing body from the pile of Texas Ranger dead at the mission. Allison's position was going to be difficult enough without restoring the "vanished spirit" fantasy as Apache subject matter. "What happened was that you fell captive to some very evil men. Do you know them in your mind now?"

She shook her head, some weariness in the frown now. "*Dah*, no," she denied. "I know we came to Old Campground, and nothing more. Just darkness then."

I knew what it was: she did not want to remember.

But there was no time to probe further with her. Juh was there, and the trip up the cliff had not helped his head from the mescal of Waiting

Camp; if glaring would mortify human tissue, Father Alvar Nunez would have been decomposed on the spot.

I murmured, "*Buenos días*, Jefe. *Qué día*," but Juh was in no mood to be told what a great day it might be, or even bid a nominal good morning.

"*Callate*," he snapped. "Come on with me."

By now, of course, we were surrounded by the people. Many of them knew me, a few were pleased to admit it, more chose to hold back. It was notable that the old ones were more friendly, the young almost hostile. I made a leap in my mind from this that the stranger had spread his ideas more successfully among the youth. That is to say the young adult warriors, not the children. I had plied too many of the very young with sweetmeats and trinkets at the mission. They welcomed me like an old friend, followed me into the rancheria as so many goslings attached to a bachelor gander.

But within the camp, drawing near a patently new jacal, quite the largest one I had seen constructed by Apaches, Juh ordered the youngsters to stay back. We went on to the big jacal, unattended.

Try as I might on this brief walk, I had not been able to discern the whereabouts of either Ben Allison or Little Buck. Both had been led away by guards on first arrival through the defile and, in the general confusion of the greeting, I had lost them. I thought to ask Juh about them but decided better. With Apaches, the less that was said, the more that might be learned.

Juh had now halted at the deerhide doorhanging of the jacal. As it was a warm morning, the hide was hung aside. A plainly foreign voice called to us from the interior to enter. We did so, and I was immediately struck by two most startling revelations. The jacal possessed a window—unheard of in Apacheria—and, seated by the light of that window, writing at a desk, which must have been freighted up the Zig Zag Trail dismantled, was one of the handsomest men my eyes had ever beheld: most striking because so young and yet, *the one.*

He arose, with a slight bow to me, waved a slender hand to the room's second chair—actual settlement furniture again—and said, surprising me with a classically Castilian accent, "Ah, Padre Nunez. *Usted es muy amable. Siéntese usted, por favor.*"

"*Un millón de gracias,*" I mumbled, unable to remove my gaze from him, feeling awkwardly for the chair.

To be recognized and greeted by name, to be told I was too kind, to be requested then to please be seated, well, it was an experience of rarity. Particularly in the context of the nature of the man who extended the gratuities. He was, after all, the most unusual furnishing of this most fantastic of Apache jacals.

Mutely, I accepted the chair.

"*Cómo le va*, Padre?" he said. "Have they treated you well?"

"*Si, muy bien, gracias.*"

He returned behind the desk and sat down again. In the brief movements he had made since my arrival, I had detected something familiar. Now, in the ramrod way that he held himself in the desk chair, I knew what it was. This man had been a soldier, and not just a *gente* of the ranks. An officer, surely.

"*Capitán*," I said, employing a small waist-bow of my own, "it is you who are too kind, and I who must inquire of you yet another kindness: you are, *de seguro*, who you must be. Of a certainty we both can admit that. But true names are another thing. You possess the advantage of me."

"As was my design, Padre." A subtle chill crept over the young face. "But be easy one moment more."

He spoke to Juh, standing soundlessly behind me, and, not looking at the man as he spoke to the chief, one could not have detected that it was not one Nednhi discoursing with another. His command of the Apache tongue was uncannily perfect. Having heard his Spanish, and now his Indian tongue, I knew of course that he was not only a soldier but a linguist of high art. Yet it was not alone Juh's language he commanded. Juh wheeled and went about his orders like some young horsetender out on his first war mission. And by that I knew that Kaytennae had been correct: there was a great and serious trouble among the Nednhi, and it was this slender *extraño* of the big jacal—the man, unquestionably, who had penned and sent the ransom demand to Governor Buckles and the military of Texas—who would now and swiftly, my every instinct told me, reveal himself *and* his damnable plan.

But he would toy with me first.

"May we speak English, Father Nunez?" he asked unexpectedly. "I have sent Juh for the Texan and the boy. It will be easier for us all. Does it present any problem for you, sir? My people tell me you are proficient in three tongues."

"Four," I corrected him.

"Ah, yes! I had forgotten. But you are no usual monkish priest. One could not look at you and imagine a tongue of Caesar's to issue forth."

"Nor would one study your face by jacal light and expect to hear such sounds as are growled in guttural by Juh, Geronimo, Mangas, and Cochise."

"Ah, yes," he said. "My face."

The charm was gone. The graceful ease evaporated. *De buenas a primeras,* all of a sudden, he was not the same. And I knew that my remark, all unintended, had reminded him not of who, but of what, he was.

He spoke no further word until Allison and

the Texas boy were brought before him. Then he waited deliberately to watch the captive Tejano's startlement to see a man of his kind in the jacal of He Who Has The Plan.

Allison reacted even more poorly than had I. He stared at the man and stared at him.

So, too, did Little Buck Buckles.

Finally Allison stammered, "*You're* him?"

The other's answer was a single, blank-eyed nod, and the quiet extended itself unbearably.

It remained for the innocently cruel candor of an eight-year-old child to make honest men of us all.

"Why, blame it all, Reverend," Little Buck complained indignantly to me, "this here feller's a nigger."

21

Flicker told us his story then. And even the boy said no other word until he had finished.

His full name was Robert E. Lee Flicker, and that was in itself where the tale of his life began. His father, James Flicker, known as Black Jim, had been one of Lee's slaves freed when Marse Robert went off to fight for the Confederacy. As was common with the blacks of the Arlington plantation, Black Jim loved the gentle man and would not accept emancipation. He followed Lee into the war, continuing to serve on his staff unofficially, indeed, anonymously. During the long and cruel years of the conflict, Black Jim managed to slip home to Arlington and visit his wife and child, the boy then, or rather at war's outset, a bright lad of fifteen. With the surrender at Appomattox, Lee insisted that Black Jim take his freedom. Jim agreed but, in the parting, told the famed Confederate commander that his one wish was that his son, now nineteen years of age, could be a soldier as General Lee was. When Lee asked the faithful Negro what, precisely, he meant in this request, James Flicker told him that it was that a black man might go to West Point—that is, that the son of a black man might do so—and graduate an officer and gentleman, "the same as any white man's son."

Lee, to the consternation of his several advisers, told Flicker that he would do what might be done.

No one at Arlington, or in Washington for that matter, expected the appointment to see reality, but it had.

Robert E. Lee Flicker, born a slave and the son of a born slave, became a black cadet at West Point.

The times at the military academy were not easy ones for any youth, least of all for a freed slave. The body of appointees was still made up of Southerners, and these youngsters were in no sense prepared to accept equality with a black boy. Young Flicker had prevailed. The memory of his father's dream carried him on. The elder Flicker had lived long enough to see his son enter the academy and stay the ensuing bitter but deeply rewarding years to the very eve of graduation. Now Robert Flicker was about to become Lieutenant R. E. L. Flicker and, with Black Jim but a fortnight in the grave, no power on earth, save his own death, could have deterred young Robert, or indeed, turned him from the path.

Then it happened.

In the dark of the final night of prom week, a young white girl, guest of an Alabama cadet of patrician but war-ruined family, had been assaulted sexually. Incoherent at the time, and failing in emotional recovery subsequently, the young woman was never permitted to testify. Her affidavit stated only that her attacker had been hooded and gloved, thus unidentifiable except by his cadet uniform. A suspect, however, was not long in being provided. Each young gentleman of the class was accounted for, either by senior officer or by agreement of fellow cadets. Except one. Robert E. L. Flicker could find no cadet to testify as to his whereabouts during the time involved. Indeed, the only testimony was from his cadet roommate, cadet captain and honor student, Jefferson Flowers, the fiancé of the victim. Said young Flowers: "I couldn't imagine where he was, and still stoutly maintain he would not and could not be guilty of such a heinous crime against a white woman. Yet circumstances force me to confess, gentlemen, that he was not in our quarters during that time when I pray to God Almighty that he had been."

The precise opposite, according to Flicker, had been the case: he, Flicker, had been in the room; Flowers had not.

But this was not, either by the trial officers or by Flicker himself, considered evidence that might in any way suggest deeper investigation of the white cadet. Such a possibility was unimaginable. Southern honor alone would forbid it. But in this matter there was much more than that to deny the unthinkable—it was Flowers' betrothed, his own bride-to-be, who had suffered the rape. The officers of the board of investigation proceeded not a single question beyond this ironclad exclusion-by-sanity of Cadet Captain Jefferson Flowers from pressing inquiry.

As for almost-lieutenant of the army, Robert E. Lee Flicker, he could thank a just and generous God that he had been appointed to the academy by General Lee and that, in accordance with this fact, together with the lack of prima facie evidence to convict him beyond peradventure of justice miscarried, he would be granted the military charity of a sergeant's rank in the enlisted corps and no formal dismissal from either the army or the United States Military Academy at

West Point. The saving appearance of the matter would be that the course had proved beyond his capacities and that, graciously, the service had offered him its shelter and succor "as a fellow soldier in time of greatest need and trouble."

The damnable thing was that young Flicker had to accept the lie and to live with it.

Any other course at all would have involved General Lee and, through him, the memory of James Flicker and Black Jim's dream.

The army had promptly sent him as far as it could.

Sergeant Robert Flicker had arrived at Fort Bliss barracks, Post of El Paso, only the year before our meeting with him in Juh's Stronghold.

But that year had been a fateful one.

Owing to his remarkable command of languages, Sergeant Flicker was assigned to the cavalry, just then engaged in a series of illegal forays into Mexico for the purpose of hot pursuit of raiding Apaches or for gathering intelligence against future raids by the hostile red men. In the course of this duty, Flicker learned not only the tongue of Juh's wild people, but much of their ways. He came to admire them and to believe he understood why they would not, or perhaps it was that they could not, surrender to the white man. At the end of six months duty in the far Southwest, Sergeant Flicker was aware of the first real stirring within him of the idea that was to lead to his eventual desertion—his longing to live as the Indians lived, wild and free, masters of their own fates as well as of the manner in which they died, and survived. At the time, he put the feeling aside as unworthy of a loyal army regular. The Indian was the enemy.

The summer passed in this way, with one welcome new addition to the lonely post life of Robert E. L. Flicker; the Negro sergeant fell in love.

The girl was the teen-aged daughter of the post sutler, a lovely thing born of her white father's illicit romance with a Lipan, or Texas Apache, woman.

The sutler, Bert Thompson, was a man of his times. Of middle years and a saving Scot's nature, he was neither a good nor a bad man but only the victim of his era's prejudgments and discriminations. Although he would admit of his fathering the half-breed girl, he would not go so far as to "Christianize" a heathen squaw—his name for Luana's mother, a stoic Lipan woman working in the post store as a laundry and cleaning domestic. Neither would he, when he learned of his daughter's interest in the young soldier, consent to Luana going on with the Negro trooper.

"It ain't anything personal, mind you," he told the young cavalryman. "I just don't want no horse soldiers fooling around with her. She's just a baby."

Privately, in fact quite publicly, he told a

different story. “No damned colored man is going to stick his black pecker into my daughter!” was his outraged cry; and Flicker, knowing the rules governing his race, understood that, once again, he had been found guilty and sentenced to banishment.

But this time he did not bend to the rule; he risked, instead, the full danger of breaking it: he continued to see the girl by dark and by devious trysting places and, as summer waned, came to know, with equal qualms of panic and warmest love, that he would be a father.

Luana and he discussed this wonderful and threatening new factor and, as so many star-crossed lovers before them, decided to let the future disclose their proper course, doing nothing the while.

It was into this uneasy peace of continuing chanceful meetings and passionate embraces “down by the summer-warm Rio Grande,” that fate sent the unkindest hurt of all.

A new officer was assigned from the East to command the troop of which Flicker’s scout patrol was the essential heart. The new man’s name? Lt. Jefferson Flowers.

A more wicked turn of blind fate could not have come to pass. Flowers, discovering Flicker’s presence in his new command, became as a man possessed. Instead of time having mellowed his memories of his black roommate, Flowers’ mind seemed to have become completely poisoned. Flicker learned that the fiancée had sickened in her mind from the attack and that Flowers had gallantly married her nonetheless, only to have the poor creature put a pistol to her head within the month to make him a widower before even the wedding couch had cooled. The bereaved officer had told the same story at that time that he told the Negro sergeant upon arriving in El Paso: it was that the girl had suddenly remembered the man who had raped her and, remembering him, could not live with the shame of having been violated by a black man fearing, as the memory returned to her, that the child she knew she was carrying within her would prove to be that of the bestial Robert Flicker.

When the lieutenant told this gross perversion of any possible truth to his sergeant-of-scouts, Flicker knew he was lost. For whatever reason that twisted the mind of Jefferson Flowers, an innocent Negro was going to be crucified in order to justify and dignify the suicide of a white woman whom that Negro had never even seen. In the ensuing seizure of desperate panic, Flicker could think of but one rational way in which he might convince the hollow-eyed white officer that he suffered a delusion about his ex-roommate's guilt of any crime involving the lieutenant's late wife. Flicker would tell Flowers about his own love for Luana Thompson and ask the white officer's understanding, in a forgiving God's name. Flicker had found a new life and wanted to let the dead past remain in peace.

To his enormous relief, Lieutenant Flowers responded to the plea with unexpected sympathy, even implied apology. He did not directly recant the falsehood of his accusation against Flicker in the death of his young wife, but definitely gave the Negro sergeant to believe that such retraction lay in the very near offing.

The first warning Flicker had to deny this naked lie was when he did not find Luana the next evening at their secret riverside meeting place. Returning to ask Bert Thompson of her where-abouts, the sutler had told the sergeant that the girl had gone "down by the river to watch the moon rise" with the new young officer, Lieutenant Flowers. And more than that. The lieutenant had winked at Thompson and told him to "be ready to announce an engagement any minute now." Naturally, Flicker would understand from that the same that Thompson had: the engagement would be that of the dashing cavalryman and Miss Luana Thompson, daughter of Mr. Albert A. Thompson, Post of El Paso.

In wounded lover's fury, Flicker saw the girl the following night. She weepingly denied any knowledge of an engagement, insisted she had gone to the river only to "hear how the grand people lived." The lieutenant had been very kind.

There had been no familiarity, no talk even of such a thing. No, he had not asked to see Luana again. Yes, of course, she promised not to see him again. Now, would Flicker take her in his arms and make everything as it had been before this foolishness?

Flicker of course had done that.

For that night happiness returned.

But only for that night.

With the dawn of next day, the girl's violated body was found "down by the river," where she and Sergeant Flicker were known to go. The young sergeant had heard the news from an Indian worker at the post. The Indian had heard it in Juárez, coming over the bridge to work that daybreak. Flicker, not waiting for any more trials by military tribunal, much less civilian hanging juries, went out of the noncommissioned officers barracks by the rear window in the gray light of early morning. Reaching the river, he went into the bottom-land brush and upstream a long way, crossed over and stole a horse and rode the entire day into Mexico. He believed, with nightfall and final failure of his mount, that he was seventy-five miles south of the international border. Stealing another horse, he rode the night through, guiding on the stars and by certain landmarks that he had learned in his scouting, to make for Casas Grandes and the Sierra Madre of the North.

Here, the principal narrative ended.

Flicker sat silent for several moments, and neither Allison nor I felt called to say a word. Juh, without instruction, took Little Buck and left the jacal. The Negro deserter roused up as if from a medicine trance.

"I have not recounted this story to anyone else," he told the Texan and myself. "What would be the use?"

He shook his head, pausing again.

"They would not believe me, as you have not believed me. If a man is black, nothing else can alter the judgments made against him. This is equally true if the jury be Anglo or Mexican. I am sure, Father," he said to me, "that you understand the truth of this."

I nodded that I did, and he continued.

"Now we come to the difficult part. Do I understand that you still have the document I prepared which I instructed Juh to leave with you?"

"*Si*, *Capitán*," I said, then frowned. "How do you wish to be called?" I asked him. "Have you a preference?"

He gave me a quizzical, brief stare. "How would you call me if I were white?" he countered.

I had not thought of it and admitted as much. "However," I guessed, "I suppose I would call you as I call Allison here. I would call you simply Flicker."

"Do it then."

"Yes, but you do not call me simply Nunez."

"Sergeant Flicker, then, Father Nunez."

He looked at me, dark face clouding.

"Now we come to the ugliness, eh?" he said. "The ransom note properly delivered should be reaching the authorities in Texas this same morning. Instead, either you or your white friend has it on his person here in this mountain camp of my people." His smoldering eyes found both the Texan and myself, searching us with a common glance.

"*My* people," he repeated. "The new *Chihuahuenos*."

Allison and I nodded instinctively.

"The paper," he said. "Give it to me."

"But you don't understand," I delayed. "It has been left behind at the mission. For safekeeping, Sergeant."

I could see his face tighten and knew he would challenge the lie. By supreme will, I prevented my eyes from appealing to Allison for help. "God's Name, Flicker," I said impulsively, "do you know that 'sergeant' sounds no more correct to me than simply Flicker. May I make another suggestion? I would like to call you *teniente*."

"Lieutenant?" he said, with warning softness. "Why?"

"Because, when first I saw you, I said to myself, there is a soldier; no, more than that, he is an officer surely. That is God's truth, Flicker."

"Yes it *is* God's truth, Father. But I don't want to hear that rank spoken again to me. My name is Robert Flicker. You had better remember that."

"It is not permitted then to call you by the rank you have bravely earned?"

"It would change nothing. Must I warn you again?"

"Ha!" I snorted. "Calling me a bishop would not elevate me, either. But I relish the sound of it."

He did not answer but turned to his solitary window and stood staring out of it. At last, he said to us, still not turning from the window, "I don't know what to do with you. Go and clean yourselves up. Rest if you wish, or wander about the camp. You have the freedom of the rancheria."

He raised his voice, calling Juh, and the Nednhi chief entered. Flicker repeated the instructions he had furnished us, except to add an Apache proviso.

"If either of them moves to get away," he said, "kill them both."

22

Juh remanded us to the custody of Kaytennae.

It was then just after eleven in the morning.

One may imagine we were not sleepy. The ascent of the great cliff may have wearied our muscles but our minds were alert to our position.

As to that, Allison rated it a *camino cerrado*, a dead-end trail. We would try to discuss it as quickly as we might be rid of our young guard. Fortunately, Kaytennae helped out here. He wanted to go and see his aunt Huera, he said, and warned us to try nothing, as he would be away no longer than a pack mule required to stale. We promised to wait quietly where we were, on the knoll above the warrior woman's wickiup. He departed on the hurried trot.

"All right, Padre," Allison said. "It's tally time."

We had the ransom note. It was hidden in the sweatband of his flat black hat. But it meant nothing. It had no power. Flicker could write another in five minutes. Forget the note. What of Juh and the Nednhi then? Strike them also. They would be what Flicker led them into being. We were back to the black deserter.

What of him?

He meant to try us by the Mexican law, Allison said. He was speaking of the *ley fugue*, the "shot while attempting to escape" rule of the *Juaristas* and *ruralistas*.

I demurred, incensed. Whatever he was, poor fellow, Robert Flicker was no killer.

Allison admitted my championing of the colored man touched him deeply. Nevertheless, he insisted, he himself would continue to fret about a way out of that Apache encampment *alive*. I was forgetting that Flicker was a wanted murderer, whether guilty or not. He could not afford to free us, nor risk our making an escape, nor give the Nednhi time to remember what they owed Father Nunez. We were not, he assured me, an even-money bet to "make it home with our hair on." Not that Apache springtime.

"Mr. Robert E. Lee Flicker is sooner or quicker going to tell these here 'Paches of his to give us a two-jump head start and commence firing," Allison concluded. "That's as sure as bullets bring blood."

"Never!" I cried. "He is a man of culture, of great dignity, whom life has cruelly used and who, in this pristine solitude, with these untutored but honorable children of nature, has at last found a home. I pray for his happiness, and for theirs."

The big Texan bobbed the flaxen mane of his hair, pulled down the wide brim of his black hat.

"Whilst you at it, Padre," he said, "throw in a Hale Marie for our side, too, will you?"

"Hail Mary," I corrected stiffly.

"You bet," he said. Then, pointing suddenly, "Speaking of your colored friend finding himself a better hole to hide in, lookit yonder. Ain't that him a-striding all hot and bothered down to Huera's wickiup?"

It was Flicker, of course, and at first I did not identify the flush that spread over me. Allison's eye caught it, however.

"Son of a gun, Padre," he said. "You're jealous."

This was total pig-swill, a reductio ad absurdum of most flagrant sort, and I shouted as much back at him.

"Plumb center!" he crowed delightedly. "Bang!"

I would not stand for this and stomped away from him. There is nothing so irritating to an educated human being as the truly simple mind.

There is also, at times, nothing so devastatingly able to see the truth.

Kaytennae came back to us with fearful proof. He had been dismissed when Flicker arrived at Huera's wickiup but had not come back to us immediately. Rather, he had idled at the rear of the brush hutment in seeming delay to repair a rip in his moccasin. Sitting on his rock seat, there behind the wickiup, no more than twenty feet from its thin walls, he could hear every word spoken therein.

It was those words that now so deeply troubled Kaytennae.

"Blackrobe Jorobado," he said, "I owe you a life. When I was but a boy I had the brain fever caught from horses, and you cured me of it. Now I would return you that life, but do not know how to do so."

Ben Allison instantly sensed the deadliness here.

"Begin by telling us what you heard down there," he broke in tersely. "*Más pronto*, hombre."

I was certain the youth would comply as instructed except that now, of a seeming sudden, we had been discovered by the other youngsters of the camp and an entire horde of them, complete with one pet deer, three camp burros, and a tame raven, was bound up the rise to join us. Kaytennae rose to the need. With adult Apachean hauteur, he told the rabble that his orders were to keep Blackrobe Jorobado and the tall Tejano *pistolero* apart from all in the rancheria, especially curious and troublesome children. "*Ugashe*!" he shouted at the button-eyed starers. "Back to your mothers!"

The little ones did not raise any dust departing, but they did straggle off, and Kaytennae continued.

"The black one, He Who Has The Plan," he said, "has told my aunt that the wonderful new Winchester guns are a sign from Ysun that the plan must go forward. A new ransom note will be sent off with sunrise. Imagine, he told her, if only ten new Americano rifles could kill nine Texas Rangers and defeat a company of Mexican cavalry, think what might be done with all the new Americano rifles in the arsenal at Post of El Paso? That is why he nearly ran to see my aunt. She must bless any change of venture, as she blessed the first El Paso raid. And the black one has told her *this is the time*." Kaytennae paused, frowning. "There is another bad thing, too."

"Wonderful," Allison nodded. "Just what we need."

"I think I know something even Juh does not suspect," the Apache youth persisted. "I think

He Who Has The Plan is in love with my aunt."

"Bah!" I cried, flushing again. "You have been listening beneath too many ramada thatches!"

"But I listened well, Blackrobe."

"Rascal! You should be flogged."

"Hold up, Padre." It was Allison, of course, returning to realities. "We'd best hear the rest of what the kid has to say. You got to remember that Flicker hooked me and you to the same whiffletree. Happen this 'Pache catch-colt of yours means to lead you out of these here Nednhi bulrushes, I go along."

I had in truth forgotten the black soldier's instruction to shoot us both in case of trouble with one. Apologizing to Kaytennae, I urged him to continue. He did so, but palpably nervous now. He kept throwing anxious glances toward the wickiup of Huera the Blonde. I could see the perspiration bead his sensitive face, and I took heed: when an Apache sweats, wise Mexicans and white men will look to every possible exit from the vicinity.

23

Kaytennae addressed himself to me, but I watched Ben Allison: I wondered how he would feel now about killing every Apache in Juh's El Paso war party, having found this brave young friend among that party's number?

The youth began by saying that his uncle had been initially lured to steal the Texas white boy by the promise of the black soldier that they could exchange the boy for a ransom of all the new rifles in the American arsenal at Post of El Paso. And the black one had said that these new rifles were the wonderful kind, called Spencers, that had the short barrels, were loaded through the buttstock, and would shoot seven times at the flick of the lever.

Some Nednhi had been skeptical at first but Juh had won them over. Now all the Apache bands of the Chiricahua praised the great, bold adventure. Nana, Victorio, Mangas, Eskiminzin, Loco—even the wild young Bedonkohe, Geronimo—were reported ready to follow Juh and the mysterious black *extraño.*

However, the black soldier had not taken so generous a view of the warchief's success. Juh had done too many things wrong. He had killed all those Texas Rangers. He had done too much talking up in the Davis Mountain camps of the Texas Lipan chief, Magoosh. Little doubt he had let slip the identity of the fugitive black man inhis Mexican stronghold whose plan it was to kidnap the son of the Texas governor. Those Lipans would have reported this to the officers at Fort Bliss. American cavalry and Texas Ranger volunteers alike might even then be riding for Casas Grandes. The entire plan could be imperiled.

All of this, Kaytennae now concluded, he had just reviewed with his aunt Huera. It was why he had left us, to plead with her for our safety. She had seemed sympathetic, perhaps realizing at last that she owed her life to the Tejano, Al-li-sun. But Kaytennae could not be sure.

At that point where he would have asked his aunt to tell him if she would join in helping him free the prisoners—all of them, Little Buck, Blackrobe Jorobado, *and* the tall one with the pale eyes—the black one had come hurrying down from his big jacal.

And that was where the trail for Kaytennae's two friends, and the white boy they had risked their lives to rescue from the Apache, now grew dark and dim.

It was made that way by what Kaytennae had heard while feigning the moccasin repair behind the wickiup of Huera the Blonde; and what he had heard was that the black one had a new plan.

Well, not really a new plan.

A delay in the old one.

The black one had convinced Huera that Juh had put them all in danger by his faulty leadership. The only way that Juh might now redeem himself would be to personally battle the one who had brought the warchief to a humbling before his own war party. A committee of three warriors who had been on that raid—standard procedure among the Nednhi in war business—

had been appointed to consider the matter of their leader's failures. Their verdict, only now brought to He Who Has The Plan: Juh must fight and kill the Tejano Allison.

But wait; that would merely restore Juh to a warrior's place among the Nednhi, a matter of personal honor as an Apache fighting man shamed by a Pinda Lickoyi, a damned pale-haired White Eye and, worse yet, one from the hated Texas country.

As to who would be the future war leader of the Nednhi, He Who Has The Plan sought from Huera, the holy woman of the band, the warrior woman whose spirit-words were law in the stronghold, her own vision of that man upon whom this crucial honor would now fall.

Here, our teller-of-tales put out his hands in helpless gesture to us both.

"I am sorry for you, my friends," Kaytennae said, "but more of sorrow is within me for my aunt."

"Your aunt, boy?" Ben Allison broke in sharply. "What about her? Has that feller done her harm?"

"No, no, Al-li-sun," he said, pronouncing the name syllabically, as did Juh and the others, "she has done him an honor."

"Ah, no," I breathed, guessing the tragedy.

"Ah yes, Blackrobe," Kaytennae nodded, "he is the new warchief of the Nednhi."

24

In the pause that greeted Kaytennae's revelation, Allison and I saw past the boy to where the fringe of the timber bordered the meadowland. This was up from our knoll above Huera's wickiup a matter of only thirty paces. Up there, coming out of the trees, was the powerful figure of Juh. Kaytennae, reading our faces, did not move to swing around. "Who is it coming there?" he asked. "My uncle?"

Allison nodded, but said nothing.

"How did you know?" I asked.

"If you are talking of someone and what you are saying is bad, he feels it."

"Nonsense, he is here to see that you are doing your job of watching us."

Kaytennae did not answer, and Juh drew up to us.

The mescal was not in him any last bit now. His huge face seemed drawn. There was more of sadness than of menace in his air. He appeared beaten.

Kaytennae's face reflected the change.

"You have heard then, uncle?" he said.

"Yes. But I don't believe it. Do you, nephew?"

"I must believe it; our aunt told me."

"To your face? And you did not come to warn me?"

"It was not to my face. I overheard it from outside her wickiup, when he sent me away. As for coming to warn you, I had your own orders to guard these prisoners."

Juh nodded. "*Enjuh.* Perhaps you thought if you left them, I might shoot them as he ordered?"

"No. You would not do that."

"*Enjuh*, boy. You know me better than I know myself."

"Perhaps it is that I love you better than you love yourself, uncle."

Again Juh nodded, again shook his head frowningly.

"I still don't believe it," he said. "Why would the black one turn against me? It was his plan. No, I won't think ill of him. He has brought us too much hope and made us feel like men again. He won't do this thing to me."

But Juh was wrong.

"Uncle," Kaytennae told him, low voiced, "do not humble yourself to turn and stare, but three men come now from the big jacal. They look this way and they are bound this way."

"The committee? Already? No!"

"Uncle, they're coming here."

"Who is it? Give me their names."

"Sunado. Keet. Nazati."

I watched the warchief, knowing these names myself. They were good fighters and bad men to make argument with. They were also Juh's favored drunken friends, as I well knew from the frequent trips of the quartet to the cantina of my parishioner Elfugio Ruiz, in Casas Grandes. But all that Juh did was to heave a great sigh and murmur, "All my good friends."

Sunado, Keet, and Nazati stopped a respectful ten feet away. "Jefe," Sunado said, "we have all met with him. We don't like it, but we are the committee for your preparation. What do you think?"

Juh would not face them.

"If men who rode with me have voted against me, I do not think anything; it is the law."

"Will you resist?" asked the second man, Keet.

"No."

"*Enjuh*," Keet said. "Does the Tejano know of the law?"

"Ask him."

"He knows," Kaytennae offered. "He will fight."

"It will be at sunset," Nazati said.

"Al-li-sun will be ready," volunteered Kaytennae.

At this point, the Texan, not content to be represented by a stripling among grown men, objected.

"Jefe," he complained, indicating Kaytennae, "can you not send this *ish-ke-ne* away? This is a grave matter. It concerns only you and me."

"I like to hear the boy talk," Juh scowled.

“Well, if that is the Apache way,” Allison shrugged. “Among the Comanche, boys do not talk. Neither do women. Men talk.”

“Are you saying men do not talk among my people, Tejano?”

“I don’t know, Jefe. Go ahead, boy. Your uncle wants to hear your opinion in this serious business.”

“Bah!” Juh exploded. “Will you get out of here, Kaytennae. Go and help your near-mother, that oldest wife of mine, to take care of that white cub. He has bitten her two times already and run away from her both times. You can run faster. Besides, don’t hang about men all the while. I’ve told you that!”

I thought to see just the trace of a grin on young Kaytennae’s face, but he left immediately, trotting to be gone, and of course I must have been mistaken. I did not imagine, however, the simple keenness with which Ben Allison had gotten the boy out of harm’s way.

But Texans are forever overdoing a thing.

“Kaytennae!” Allison called out. “Tell Little Buck to be of high spirits. The Nednhi are people of their word, absolutely. No harm will come to him as long as Juh remains chief. Tell him that.”

Surely now he had gone too far.

Juh roused up from his apathy. He stormed up to the Texan and stood with him *nariz a nariz*, nose on nose. “What is that you say, Tejano?

‘As long as Juh remains chief’? I do not like the sound of that.”

“*Dispénseme*, Jefe,” the Texan murmured, “I thought you knew. I thought they had told you *all* of it.”

He gestured to Sunado, Keet, and Nazati, who scowled and moved about most uneasily. And now, at last, Juh whirled about to face the hang-dog trio.

“What is this that you have not told me?” he demanded, the bear’s voice growling deep again. “There is something here you dared not say to your warchief. Say it now!”

His hand went to his knife.

In answer, the three Winchester rifles of the committee made loud clicks as their hammers were cocked.

“Don’t be a fool!” warned Sunado.

Keet and Nazati added their nods, thumbs hooked over rifle hammers. “Huera has ruled it,” said one of them.

The mention of the warrior woman slowed Juh.

His hand dropped away from the blade.

“What has she ruled?” he asked.

“There will be a new war leader of the Nednhi named tonight. After you fight the Tejano.”

“Well, of course,” waved Juh, relieved. “When I have killed Al-li-sun, who would—” He stopped in mid-speech, to stare at the three committee-men.

"Win *or lose,*" Sunado told him, "there will be a new leader."

It was then that Juh knew where the dangerous game of tribal power had brought him.

He ignored his three attendants to stare across the encampment toward the big jacal of Robert Flicker.

"Get out of my way," he said to the three. "I am going up there right now."

Sunado, Keet, and Nazati stood aside.

"That is right, Jefe," Sunado said. "And we are going up there right behind you."

Juh strode off, never looking back at them. It was as though he had not heard Sunado. But he had heard him. He knew it was not an honor guard they marched in his rear, all that wordless way across the rancheria that had been his before the black soldier came.

25

In the kingdom of Juh, Tulapai was queen.

Named for the potent corn-mash liquor brewed by the Nednhi, Tulapai loved the spiritous life. Indeed, she was next only to Juh in her enjoyment of the jug. Some among the band said the eldest wife of the warchief had originally been called Antelope Child, and that Juh had rechristened her in honor of her skills in the fermentation of his favorite potable. Gazing upon the beauteous Antelope Child in the present, full flower of her reign over the house of the warchief, one might be forgiven the thought that Juh had chosen well in the matter of her name: his first love did more closely resemble a jug of tulapai than the fawn of the graceful pronghorn.

Tulip, as she was known in Casas Grandes, was ugly, short, broad of beam, dark and pocked of hide, enormous of head, with a mouth that seemed to open as a traveler's purse, wide enough to engulf the world in its unexpected, indeed spectacular, sunburst of a smile.

She was beyond all Apache question the happiest in heart among the four Chiricahua bands.

Nothing daunted Tulip.

Not even Little Buck Buckles.

I discovered this now as I came, seeking sanctuary, up to the wickiup of the old wife.

"*Hija mía*!" I cried in genuine relief. "It is a thing of pure joy to see that you are at home."

"Blackrobe," she laughed, "you do not fool me; what do you want? But no, wait, that is an ungracious thing to say to a poor humpbacked priest. Forgive it. I am as glad to see you as you to see me. This damned white boy is destroying my household. You can see where he is."

I could indeed. Little Buck was tethered outside the wickiup on a dog stake, with an ancient

Spanish slave iron locked about his middle and running by a rusted length of chain to a three-foot hard pine "spike" malleted into the rocky ground.

However, he was not muzzled, and he greeted me with the same fervor as when first he aided me in the dangerous matter of saving the life of Ben Allison from the Nednhi scalpers during the Texas Ranger killing.

"By Tophet, Reverend!" he yelled out. "It's abouten time you showed up. Where's old Ben Allison?"

"*Chitón*, *hijo*!" I ordered him. "In God's Name, be quiet. I am trying to find a place to hide."

Even as I spoke, Tulip found the back of my frock with a hand the size and tenderness of a mummified ham and literally hurled me into the wickiup, where I would be safely out of village view. She then picked up a rock, not a small one either, and shied it at Little Buck on the end of his dog chain. She did not miss, and the Texas boy yelped like a cur well hit.

"You heard the blackrobe," Tulip smiled. "Be a good boy."

Little Buck, rubbing his abused buttock, growled something not in dog language which astonished me for its mature evil. Tulip laughed outright.

"You hear him, Blackrobe?" she cried, entering the wickiup and seating herself across the fire-spot from me. "That's a man-child! I wish Ysun had been so kind to me. But I will make him Apache, inside and outside. He will be the true son of Juh and Tulapai. Shut up, boy."

Lowering her voice, she stared intently at me.

"What is it, Blackrobe? Why are you alone? What has happened to the tall one? Say, do you know that if I were twenty summers younger, I would buy him from Juh. He has a look to him, that big Tejano. I will bet you that his women are all with child."

"Be still, you harridan!" I chided her. "He has no woman at all. And you cannot buy him now for any price. You will be lucky to get Juh back."

This brought her into the wickiup with me.

"Go ahead," she said. "Something bad, eh. It's that damned *desertor*, isn't it, that *bastardo negro*!"

"Yes," I said and told her of the treachery of Huera against Juh and of the support of the warrior woman for the black soldier, of the placing of the warchief in camp arrest by his own men and of his march across the rancheria to see the black one.

"Ah!" she said. "Then you and the Tejano were left there for the moment unguarded, and he has made his escape. You see, priest? I told you that he was a real studhorse."

"He may be," I granted, "but he is still with the Nednhi herd. When we were alone, he did indeed think to get under cover. We made for the timber above the knoll where, as he put it, we could straighten out our brains. Just as we got to the pines, out of them stepped some more of Juh's war party. They fell on poor Allison with their rifle butts and beat him to the ground. They bound him with a horsehair riata and drove him away with kicks and quirt thongs. The last I saw of them, they seemed bound for the big jacal, after Juh and the others."

Tulip's happy nature failed.

"Who led the ones that beat the Tejano?"

"Otsai."

"Damn."

"Yes, that is a bad fellow."

"Otsai hates Juh. He always had it in his mind that he, himself, should be warchief. I warned Juh many times to kill him along a dark part of the trail. You know, Blackrobe. The way you Mexicans do it. As an accident."

"What will we do?" I asked.

"It would help if we knew where they took the Tejano."

"I'm sorry. I did not have the courage to stand there and wait to see. I could only think to remember that Juh had sent Kaytennae to stay with you, so I ran here as fast as I might." I paused. "And where is he?" I asked. "Where is Kaytennae?"

"Never mind," said Tulapai, the oldest wife of Juh. "Here." She handed me, out of the darkness, an unglazed clay jug. "Do like the Tejano said. Straighten out your brain."

"*Hija*!" I objected. "This stuff will straighten out the entire body." But I took a long and glugging pull at it, all the same. Choking, I passed it back to the eldest wife. "*Madre Dios*!" I gasped. "You have poisoned me!"

"What?" she cried. "Is it possible? It is, it is! I gave you the wrong jug. That is the one we keep the black medicine in for dipping the sheep."

"*Santissima*!" I yelled. "Carbolic?"

I fell over forward grasping belly with both hands.

So did Tulip.

Only she was dying of laughter.

"*Dispénseme*, Jorobado," she wept, when she could control the laughing, "but I could not help myself. You have always been so *puro*, such a *simplon*. Now you know we do not have any sheep. Ha, ha, ha—!"

"Curse you!" I said, recovering weakly. "How would I know you don't have any sheep? You steal anything you want, you *bárbaros*, you!"

"You will live, then, Blackrobe?"

"I don't know; I thought you were my friend."

"I had better be," the ugly woman said. "Do you know what the talk is in the rancheria? For you, I mean, Jorobado? *Dah-eh-sah*. Yes, that's what I said."

"But I am a priest!"

"So was the one who started the talk."

"No! Huera?" I could not accept it. "*She* wants me dead? *Impossible!* Ask Kaytennae. He was there, he saw it all. We saved her life, Allison and I!"

"Kaytennae has already told me. I'm sorry, Blackrobe. The boy also told me something else about his fierce young aunt; he said he saw you looking at her in the same way the black soldier does: but she hates you. She says to the people now that you are the one who freed the Tejano from the dead-pile of the *diablos* at your church. She is telling it that Allison is an evil shade and you are his master. She says that, as long as you live, Allison cannot be killed. She says therefore that Juh will die in the fight with the big Tejano, unless you are killed before the fight."

"My God!" I cried. "Wicked! wicked!"

Tulip nodded. "She is a witch of my people, Jorobado. They fear her more than any man. That's why you are in great danger here. All has changed for you."

I refused to believe it, even feeling the chill of its mere possibility settle about me in the darkness. Sensing this, Tulip said, "Only wait a little while; I have sent Kaytennae out to hear what he can of how the people feel. But I must say to you that I know already how they feel—they feel as *she* tells them to feel."

"You hate her," I accused, surprised.

“As only an old ugly woman can hate a young and pretty one,” Tulip answered. “Don’t you think that Juh, too, sees those delicious fruits she carries beneath her blouse? Bah! Hate, you say? A poor, small word for how I feel, Jorobado.”

My vision of Huera the Blonde, of my wild Apache love, whose parts I had seen at Laguna de Luz and whose heart, I had dared to imagine, might in some secret pagan way return the worship of a poor lost misshapen young priest of the Spanish Faith, ah! that vision faded now into the black, stifling gloom of the interior of Juh’s wickiup.

She was no god-woman.

She was no priestess of these innocent barbarians.

She was an Apache Delilah.

She saw the power that was in Robert Flicker, as Robert Flicker saw the power that was in Huera the Blonde. They were both bitten of the same mad dog of desire to destroy the Pinda Lickoyi, the pale-eyed Anglos of the North—to hate the white man till death did them part of their evil, twisted devotions—and if this madness meant injustice, even death, for Juh, so be it. The plan was for the people.

Fortunately for the lives of tall Ben Allison and limping Blackrobe Jorobado, one old squaw and one young warrior did not believe the plan.

They knew who the people were.

They were Juh and Tulapai and Kaytennae.

True Nednhi Chiricahua.

Not all those fools rushing to obey an Apache woman who rode and fought and lived like a man, and a black *extraño* of a soldier deserter who had lied to the Nednhi about getting five hundred guns for one small white boy.

"Do you think there is any way, Tulip," I said at last, softly, "that we may truly help the people?"

Juh's wife peered out the door of the wickiup.

"I don't know," she said. "Perhaps Kaytennae has learned something."

"He is there now?"

"Yes. He's out in the brush behind the pole corral waiting for the chance to slip in, unseen. Ah—"

As she brightened, I heard an altogether too-familiar high voice piping unwantedly, "Hey, Kaytennae! I seen you move! Where at you been? Dogs, boy, you really missed the fun!"

I heard a grunt, as of from hard throwing, and a stone the size of a Casas Grandes lemon whistled in painful ricochet off the already bruised hind end of Little Buck. "*Chito, tontito*!" hissed Kaytennae, sliding into view along the wall of the wickiup. "I won't be so nice to you next time."

"Nephew," called out Tulip, "before you come in, take the white boy for a walk on the chain. He needs to make water and perhaps dirt. Don't be long about it."

"Aunt," said Kaytennae, plainly in distress, "we must talk. Let his bladder wait."

"No, the people need to see that you are here, where Juh sent you. Show yourself. Walk the boy. But hurry. Did you learn something?"

"Everything," Kaytennae murmured. He stepped away from the wickiup and called out loudly to Little Buck, "All right, come on, *boca grande.* It is time for your walk. I will let you off the chain if you are a good dog."

"Bow wow!" answered Little Buck delightedly. "Try me out and see. I been wanting to take a pee so bad my back-jaw teeth been tasting like a buffler wailer."

I sank back against the woven-stick wall of my hiding place, too whelmed over even to pray.

What was the use? What did God know about escaping from an Apache rancheria, seven thousand feet up in the Sierra Madre of the North?

26

Kaytennae brought Little Buck into the wickiup after walking him. It was the first opportunity I had had to speak with the Texas boy at any length. It proved a fruitless gift. Little Buck was having the time of his life. Chained, rocked, yelled at, he cared not. He was "the captive" in a genuine red Indian village, and a great scalp dance and barbecue were coming up that night, at which, he had been given to understand by Kaytennae, "all hell was due to bust loose." "They was," according to young Buckles, "going to name a new chief, and old Ben was agoing to thrash the liver-lights out of the old chief and, well, by cripes, it was going to be a barn-burner."

In vain, I attempted to impart to the boy some measure of our mutual peril. If for no other reason, this was advisable to secure his cooperation in any escape that might open to us. His zestful habit of screeching out, "Hey, there, where the hell you going?" at least movement of any of us was, in itself, sufficient problem to warrant the lecturing.

It was still a waste.

He had not himself decided, he informed me, whether he would go home to Texas or stay with Kaytennae. He might also choose to stick with old Ben and become a *pistolero*. It depended. The one thing he was absolutely sure of, however, was that he had no interest whatever in becoming a priest. Or of siding-up with one. Chief on his mind was the worry that he should go to see his mother again right soon, and he wasn't sure that his Apache friends would be welcome around Fort Bliss.

Do not mistake me, the boy was no fool.

He understood that good people had died under Apache guns in the attack on the El Paso stage, an attack that would never have taken place had it not been for Little Buck Buckles being on that stage. But the boy was only eight years old. Even seeing the rangers ambushed in my garden had not deranged his emotions. Children are like that. They are not cold. They are not cruel. But death is not the same thing to them that it is to an adult. Little Buck had seen the stage crew tumble off the box. He had seen the governess shot as she ran. He had watched the Apaches fire the wrecked coach and watched them again as they took Texan hair in my mission garden. But he would still say, and mean it for the moment, that he might stay with the Nednhi. He hadn't made up his mind yet.

Well, he was an unusual boy.

Juh had noted that.

Perhaps Little Buck was a white Apache.

I only know that, in all the afternoon and until dusk drew on at sunset, where we waited in the dark of Tulip's wickiup for whatever would happen, Little Buck never once mentioned his father; nor would he be persuaded to listen to my pleas for his attention.

"Don't you fret it so, Reverend," was all he would say. "Me and old Kaytennae, we'll think of suthin."

I would learn to have more faith in Henry Garnet Buckles III, but at the moment hope and patience waned apace. "You should be birched!"

I snapped. "Were I your father, I would leave you here. Gladly!"

"Well, Reverend," he said, completely without animus, "happen you're right. But we ain't ever going to find that out, because you couldn't be my father."

"What?" I said. "Why not?"

"Because priests don't have no peckers," he told me soberly.

At first flush, I would scathe him with fire.

Then, of course, I had to laugh.

My nerves gave way and I let everything go in the roll of the laughter. Tulip and Kaytennae began first to snigger, then to guffaw. Little Buck, dirty of mind like all healthy little boys, giggled hysterically at the success of his innocent Protestant canard. In a moment we were all weeping with our cackles of relief. We were still wiping eyes and collecting mutual breath when, against the last of the sun's red light, six Nednhi men loomed suddenly in the open doorspan of the warchief's wickiup.

In their van stood Otsai, the Bad One.

"Come on with us, Blackrobe," he said. "All the good places will be taken."

I stumbled to my feet. "Good places?" I said.

"*Por supuesto*," answered Otsai. "To see the Tejano die. Up close, where the blood smells rank."

27

Where Flicker had hidden the mescal jugs, none seemed to know. Probably, he had brought them in sequestered among the various properties with which he had furnished the big jacal. In any event, not long before sundown—and the scheduled battle between Allison and the deposed Juh—the containers made their convenient appearance. A fat mule was killed and butchered for spit-roasting. The fires were laid; the women had fed and put away for the night all of the smaller children. Only those girls who had menstruated and were ready for the *goo-chitalth*, the virgin dance ceremony, and the boys who had stolen one *thlee*, one horse, from the white man, or had been in at the burning of a Mexican *casa*, might attend the night's celebration. And they would sit in the last row out and say nothing. Out there in the dark with the old people and the dogs. The Apache did not confuse such participation with permitting even the older youth a say in actual affairs of the band. Tribal power is never so given; it is always earned.

Had my own Indian countryman, Juárez, maintained a similar discipline among his "children," I would not have been suffering that particular moment of Mexican history as a fireside guest of the wild Nednhi Apache. But, alas, Benito Pablo had let his young people run uncontrolled, losing not alone North Mexico but, if the rumors we heard in the Church were true, standing to lose his revolution in the south, as well.

I had the grim thought that, had El Indio been a Chiricahuan instead of an Oaxacan Indian, I might still be safe in my sacristy at Casas Grandes.

But then I thought of huge, simple Juh, together with such of his fellows as Sunado, Keet, Nazati, and Otsai, and wrote off the entire matter in my mind; I would, on balance, prefer to be in Oaxaca.

The thought of Juh was followed by his appearance at the battle site. He came alone out of the spring darkness, in no way guarded or followed. He was, I sadly noted, carrying a clay jug in one hand, and he walked with that exaggerated dignity of the drunken man of any skin color. Yet, spying where we sat, Kaytennae, Tulip, Little Buck, and myself—with our guards—he came over to us steadily enough. Greeting me with a nod and his nephew with a pat on the shoulder, he looked over our heads to Tulip and the Texas boy.

"*Ish-ke-ne*," he said, in that unbelievably low voice, "has any harm come to you?" He spoke in Apache, and the boy frowned his puzzlement.

Juh understood, repeated the query in Spanish. "No, no," Little Buck answered happily. "*Estoy bien de salud.*" He peered up at the burly Nednhi. "But *you* don't look very well, Jefe," he said, frowning again. "Has anyone harmed you?"

"No, boy. I am Juh."

"I am glad. But where are all your friends?"

"I don't need them," Juh said. "But you could do a favor for me. You remember our brave song?"

"Why, of course, *de seguro.*"

"I would like to sing it with you, *ish-ke-ne.*"

"Cripes! You would?" Forgotten was the cowpen Spanish, the labored frowning. "Leave us give her a lick, then. Here goes—!"

Juh comprehended nothing of this response save its elevated spirit. But the moment the white boy began to sing, sweet, clear, high-pitched, the towering Apache forgot all else. His great dark Mongol face lost its haunted look. A grin, as of another small boy, replaced the injured pride. The great deep bass joined in, softly and haltingly at first, then, picking up both words and rhythm, the warchief sang out the marching tempo of Little Buck's "brave song."

> Oh, her eyes were bright as diamonds
> They sparkled like the dew;
> Her hair was black as midnight
> Dah da dah da dah da dah

You can talk about your other girls
And sing of Aurelie,
But the Yellow Rose of Texas
Is the only girl for me. . . .

Well, it was surpassing strange to hear in that time and place. *The Yellow Rose of Texas*? *Pardiez*!

Juh's mixture of Apache, Spanish, and supposed English—mimicking the white boy's lyrics—would have reduced an Anglo audience to weeping with laughter. Yet the warchief had a grand singing voice, truly thrilling in its basso profundo tones of absolute pitch. Juh had a known speech impediment which impaired his native tongue in speech, but which disappeared in song. The difference may have encouraged him to become a singer, but the fact remained, from whatever inspiration, the deep-chested barbarian sang gloriously. Little Buck, too, was a singer. And the duetting of savage basso and settlement-boy soprano, at twilight-dark in the middle of an Apache camp preparing for a scalp dance and challenge fight, was unbelievably stirring.

The Yellow Rose of Texas?

I had never heard it, or heard of it.

But I would remember it forever from that night just before the deposed Nednhi warchief and the captive Texas cowboy were to fight to see who lived.

28

Across the camp now we could see torchlights coming from the big jacal. We had little doubt of who might prove the "guest of honor" in that parade of rush-and-tallow flambeaux. But in the slight time required for the procession to wind down from Flicker's dwelling to the "plaza" of the rancheria, I had a last moment to query Kaytennae.

"Are you quite sure of what you have told me?" I whispered. "It would be a terrible thing if you were wrong."

Kaytennae checked to see if Otsai, or any of the guards, were listening. They were not. They were watching the others of our party. Juh now sat with his old wife Tulapai and the white boy, whom the warchief sheltered next to him in an arm embrace. The two were nodding to the cadence of a low, rumbling chant in Apache that Juh now intoned. Betimes, and between long notes, the warchief and his old wife were finishing off the jug of mescal. Little Buck seemed enchanted with the Nednhi couple and would not even look in our direction. Kaytennae seemed satisfied.

"I made no mistake," he told me. "You can see there are many boulders up there behind the black one's jacal. I was able to creep from the pines into those rocks and so come up beneath his prized window, which was open for the unusual heat of this day lingering. Every word came to me exactly; he speaks better in our tongue than do we. No, what I told you he said, he said."

I peered up toward Flicker's place but the darkness was down too heavily now. The boulders described by Kaytennae were only shadows upon other shadows. But the torches were much nearer now, and I could see Ben Allison walking, in his distinctive bowlegged stride that only Americano cowboys and old sea dogs practice, between two lines of Nednhi men. These, I saw, were the remaining warriors of the original raiding party that Juh had led into Texas. To my surprise, the Negro deserter was not among their number.

"Say it one more time," I instructed Kaytennae.

The young Apache nodded quickly. "Otsai, Keet, and Sunado were present. The black soldier said this final word to them: 'Juh will be drunk; he has the jug and will drink it and cannot then beat the Tejano in any fight. So he will lose and can be charged with the Law of the Ancients and either killed or driven from the band. Huera has told me of this law and it does not matter that you others have not known of it before this time. She has the power and we do not. We must obey Huera. Go now, and, when Juh is drunk enough, I will send him down to you. When the Tejano wins, Huera will appear and charge that he is an evil shade and that Blackrobe Jorobado is his master and that the one may not die except that both die. The proof will be that the Tejano defeated Juh, a thing possible only through evil. Huera will say the blackrobe has no power remaining. He has lost his *cruz.* These are all true things, my brothers.' The black one told Otsai, Keet, Nazati, and Sunado, 'I say to you only what the holy woman said to me. *Enjuh. Ugashe*!' "

Kaytennae palmed dark hands in helpless period to his hushed recital. "It is exactly as I told it to you before," he said. "Al-li-sun will die and Juh will be shamed like a whipped dog and you, Jorobado, will—" He broke off the thought in deference to my settlement softness of heart and courage. "One more thing only," he added, whether in truth or only trying to shore up my fortitude, "I may be able to help you get away. Al-li-sun is doomed. But if you come with me when I say so, when the fight is high with excitement, you may live—I know a way by foot and handholds through a secret hole in the high rock to get down from here and come to South Way not far from Old Campground."

I would have queried him further but time had gone.

Keet and Nazati had Allison up to the battle site. Sunado came over to where Otsai and the others stood or squatted behind Juh. "It is time," Sunado said, and Otsai grunted and prodded Juh with his short fighting lance and then, when the big man arose, handed him the lance and ordered simply, "Go and fight."

Juh started off, lance in one hand, jug forgotten in the other. Tulip waddled after him and took back the jug and some of the people nearby sniggered and tittered. Kaytennae uttered an Apache oath. He stepped out before these people and said to them, "Make way for the warchief, you yapping dogs," and the gigglers silenced themselves.

Allison had now been given his fighting lance and was examining it, as an old Mexican expression went, in patient haste—as a man who has just been given the *banderillas* for a very bad bull, and this man has never placed a stick before in his life and only been in the arena one time previous, when, victim to the *cerveza* and the afternoon sun, he had fallen into it over the *barricada.*

But the Texan was a fighting man, one of those rare ones who had the instinct for personal combat, be it with clubs, pistols, blades, bullwhips, or six-foot Nednhi short lances.

He and Juh met now in the center of the packed dirt of their arena. As they did so, the audience of Apache men and women drew in upon them as wet rawhide upon a smooth, hot stone. In an instant the atmosphere went from holiday *cháchara*, light crowd banter, to funereal stillness. Otsai, the referee, stood with the combatants in the final moment, explaining Huera's Law of the Ancients to Juh, and lying as nakedly to Ben Allison to say that, should the Tejano be the victor, he would be given his freedom and safe passage out of Apacheria. This, *por supuesto*, would make both men easier for Flicker. Juh would fight to avoid banishment, Allison to gain his release and his life.

Flicker would be the one true victor.

But where was the black deserter?

As if in answer to my unspoken question, the people on the far side uttered a sound of surprise. Their ranks parted to admit, not only Robert Flicker, but Huera the Blonde—walking unaided save for the black man's arm. Now it was plain. Flicker had felt he must have the holy woman present to enforce spiritually his reckless actual thinking. Without the sanction of the power represented by Huera, some among them must begin to suffer second thoughts about the degradation of Juh and the false freedom for the big Tejano and even, at the last of it, of the threatened execution of Blackrobe Jorobado somewhere in the ending of this entire murky affair. Flicker must move quickly and without flaw of hesitation. And so, too, God help me, must I!

I leaped to my feet and ran in my limping

stumble of a walk out to where tall Allison and broad Juh stood facing one another. I came up to them in the same moment Robert Flicker did, Huera slowing and left behind.

"*Nombre Dios*!" I gasped to the Fort Bliss soldier. "This is an insanity! You cannot proceed, Flicker."

"Father Nunez," he said, "I must proceed. These are my people now. They have their laws. Please."

He pushed against me gently, reluctantly.

"No!" I cried. "I will not retreat. If you will kill me, you will kill me. I stand here."

"No one is going to harm you, Father," he insisted. "Huera can be persuaded on that. These two," he gestured to Juh and Ben Allison, "are lost already. If they don't finish one another, the people will take the case themselves. Nothing must interfere with the plan I have for the Nednhi. Juh has shown he cannot be trusted. The Texan is simply persona non grata. How can I release him? How can I permit him to stay?"

"But, Flicker, good God, sir, you are a civilized human being. An officer. An educated man. These poor creatures are only simple nomads. They hate the white man *and* the Mexican. Will you now add the Negro to that grim list?"

The deserter shook his head. The handsome black face showed no emotion more clearly than that of compassion tinged with real regret.

"Father, I am committed to making a final use of my training as a soldier and leader of men. The Apaches have been treated as my people have been treated. They know the same sorrows I know. They will fight for the same thing I fight for; freedom from the white man *and* the Mexican. That is all that I ask here, all that I seek among these people. You Romans have given them slavery. Texans took away Texas from them. The Mexicans pay blood money for their scalps. I bring them something decent to die for. Can you make a sin of that, priest?"

For the first time I saw what Allison had seen in Robert Flicker from the outset—the madness in him.

There was nothing more to do. Gathering a mite of courage, I scuttled past Flicker and called to the Texan, "Allison, don't waver; we have a friend here!"

The tall San Saban touched his forehead to me in the Indian manner of respect, and shook his lean head. "Padre," he said softly, "you're daft. Look to yourself and the boy. *Hasta luego*."

Several Apache men seized me and handled me roughly aside. I did not resist and they released me to rejoin Kaytennae, with Juh's old wife and Little Buck Buckles.

"Let it begin," I heard Robert Flicker say in growling Apache. "To the end."

29

But Ben Allison never crossed lance with Juh.

The Nednhi blamed it on their god Ysun. I gave Jesus Christ credit for being saved. Others saw it in their own different ways. Little Buck cried out, "By cripes, old Ben, I knowed you'd come up with suthin!" And young Kaytennae murmured, "Blackrobe, even without your *cruz* that is strong medicine to brew."

Old Tulip, finishing off the last drop in the mescal jug, brought up some gas, smacked her lips, and suggested that, Ysun and Jesus Christ be damned, she would have to say this was a purely Apache miracle.

She was right of course.

Neither Ben K. Allison nor Friar P. Alvar Nunez had one thing to do with the uproar that now befell the Nednhi camp.

But I will still thank *my* God.

The black deserter Robert Flicker had no more than signaled the beginning of the mismatched combat, when, out of the U-notch defile of the cliff trail, burst two Indian horsemen. Their wild yelping cries—the piercing brush-wolf barkings with which the Apache traditionally warned their camps to "beware and be ready"—told every Nednhi on the mountain that a very big news-thing was being brought to the old warchief by his trusted scouts.

Yes, it was Tubac and Ka-zanni, the pair dispatched by Juh at Old Campground to trail out the fleeing Kifer and his fellow scalp hunters. The success of these scouts now wrought a stunning reversal to Flicker's demeaning of the warchief.

Ka-zanni and Tubac rode staggering ponies to the fires of the lance fight arena. They virtually fell from their exhausted mounts. But they themselves could still stand. And listen to this!

They had pushed hard after Kifer hoping to catch him and take his hair in vengeance before he might reach the safety of Casas Grandes. But Kifer was smart and he knew the mountain trails as well as any Apache. *De seguro*, all the Nednhi knew that of him. Santiago Kifer had learned from his father, and Dutch John Kifer had known things about the Sierra Madre of the North that even the Nednhi did not remember. He had surely taught Santiago where Juh's Stronghold was, and how to get up to it and back down, and listen even harder to this: that knowledge was going to prove a dangerous matter for the people within the next few suns.

Kifer and his men had run their horses all night through from Old Campground, reaching Casas Grandes with daybreak, Ka-zanni and Tubac right behind them. And what a sight that sunrise had shown all of the night riders, down there in the town!

Camped in and about the Mission of the Virgin of Guadalupe were no less than half a hundred Americano horse soldiers. Kifer quickly hid from the soldiers by going into the old adobe ruin west of the town and beside the river going up into Casas Grandes Canyon. From there, he sent a man into town. This man went to the cantina of Elfugio Ruiz and brought back the young, half-Chiricahua wife of Ruiz. The girl was known by the scalp hunters to have been the secret sweetheart of the nice blond boy named Carson who had had his head chewed off by the wolves back at Old Campground. When they told this half-breed girl what the Nednhi had done to her lover with the long yellow curls, she swore vengeance against the people of Juh and told Kifer all that was going forward in the town.

Ka-zanni and Tubac had, *por supuesto*, waylaid the simpleton girl as she was sneaking back to the cantina before old Ruiz might learn of her visit to the scalp hunter camp, and they had gotten their own story, by their own means, out of her. There could be no doubt their story matched that told Kifer.

What the Yanqui horse soldiers were doing so far down in Chihuahua State, against all Mexican law, was looking for the Negro deserter Robert Flicker and for the Apaches of the Nednhi raider

Juh, the band that had stolen the small son of the governor of Texas.

Word of that crime had come to Post of El Paso and Fort Bliss even as the black one had feared it would, from the Tejano Lipan Apaches who had reported to the fort all of Juh's hard-drinking talk in their camps. Now these horse soldiers down there in Casas Grandes were not just regular troops but were the ill-famed Apache chasers the black one had scouted for when he was a *sargento* in the Fort Bliss cavalry. And they were in Casas Grandes not just to look for Juh—they might look forever in those mighty Blue Mountains and never find one Nednhi—but they were looking for a local man to guide them into the Sierra, a man who *did* know where to seek out Juh's Stronghold, and who, for a price of blood money, would take the horse soldiers into that legend-place.

But no Casas Grandan had been eager to earn this reward.

They had to live there after the Americanos went back over the Rio Bravo, called by them the Rio Grande.

But the impasse gave Santiago Kifer a natural inspiration. He would offer, for a guarantee of United States *and* Texas amnesty for himself and his band, to take the command straightaway to Juh's Stronghold.

Suiting action to inspiration, Kifer sent down to the encampment of American cavalry a local intermediary to inquire of the young officer in command if he would parley with the scalp hunters in regard to the whereabouts of the Nednhi Apache who, led by the missing Negro sergeant, had stolen Governor Buckles' small son? Kifer's only price for the information was amnesty for his men and himself. Could a deal be made on this basis?

The officer, replying to the query, wanted to know why he should accept such an offer, when he understood from others of the Casas Grandans—specifically from Señora Elfugio Ruiz, who had relatives among the wild Apache—that the stronghold was impregnable. No, he told the intermediary, Kifer would have to come up with something firmer than just the whereabouts of Juh's hideout, and/or the guiding there.

The scalp hunter was ready for that.

He knew a place, he sent back by the same local courier, where dynamite charges could be placed, and the one trail into and out of the great mesa could be obliterated, trapping the entire tribe of the Nednhi Apache and the Negro deserter for all time—if the Americano officer would care for that solution.

However, Kifer's suggestion was that the mere conveying of this dynamite threat to the Apache would result in abject, complete, and immediate surrender. No man—and no Apache man, woman, or child—would choose starvation over

Americano capture. The Nednhi all had Americano cousins among the three other Chiricahua bands who were on the reservations up there, and they weren't starving.

So if Kifer took the officer to the stronghold, it would be all over for Juh, one way or the other.

And the officer could begin polishing up his insignia for next promotion: to bring Juh in would rank with the reduction of Geronimo, Nana, Loco, or Victorio; not to mention whatever the black deserter was worth.

It was done, they had a deal, agreed the young white officer.

Regarding the black man, he would be turned over to the Texas authorities to face a charge of murdering a young girl in El Paso. As for Juh and the Nednhi and the surrender of the son of the governor of Texas, unharmed and in good health, the officer would follow Santiago Kifer into the Sierra the first day that the hard-riding troops were rested and the supply wagons got up to Casas Grandes with the necessary explosives to implement the destruction of the Zig Zag Trail.

How long would that be? Kifer had wanted to know.

Two to four days, replied the officer. Make a guess of three days; three days from next morning, not the present one.

That had been a day and a half ago, Ka-zanni and Tubac said. They had ridden home to the stronghold in that record time to warn the people. Even so, that would mean that Juh—or He Who Has The Plan—had something only in the order of another day and a half, two full days at most, to take what action they would, flight or battle.

Here, Robert Flicker, saying not one word the entire time, stopped the panting scouts.

"*Schichobes*, old friends," he said to Tubac and Ka-zanni, "did you hear a name for the young officer?"

Tubac, the spokesman, frowned a little.

"Why, you should know him," he answered. "Isn't that your old troop you told us you scouted for?"

"Did you get a name?" Flicker said, low voiced.

"Yes, a very odd one. Pretty, though."

"Was it Flowers? Lieutenant Flowers?"

"Why, yes. You see, I told you you should know him."

"Very handsome officer," Ka-zanni offered, so that he would not be left out. "The young wife of Ruiz told me he was the kind of a man that makes the things of a woman grow warm and tingle. But we didn't see him."

The dark face of Robert Flicker looked as if it had turned to stone.

"Two days," he said, half-aloud.

"We can still catch them in Casas Grandes.

"Trap them inside the mission garden.

"Keep them in there and kill them as they

planned to kill us. Trap and starve. Let no one of them escape. When we have them wounded enough, *wagh*!"

He swung about to face the excited Nednhi crowding now all about him and the returned scouts.

"I, too, know how to use the *dinamita*!" he cried. "And we will capture it from their army wagons and use it ourselves to blow in the walls of Blackrobe Jorobado's church and his gardens, when we are ready for the last rush upon the soldiers.

"It will be the greatest of beginnings of the war of the Apache people to win Chihuahua for themselves!

"To your ponies!

"To Casas Grandes!

"*Ugashe—*!"

30

When the Nednhi broke from the lance fight fires to run for their war ponies, Ben Allison also ran. Flicker saw him go and yelled to Juh to recapture him. Juh shouted to others to stop the Tejano, but the mill of men and women and excited oldsters was too great. Ben reached Kaytennae and Father Nunez who, you may believe it surely, was praying hard that no one would begin shooting in the melee. The Texan swooped down on Tulip and Little Buck, seizing up the white boy.

"Foller me!" he ordered and went long-legging his way up the slope toward the rocks and timber. Kaytennae and I leaped to follow, but here came Huera the Blonde waving her Winchester and commanding us to halt.

Allison left Little Buck in the rocks and bounded back down the slope. Huera heard him and whirled about. The Tejano in that instant was no more than thirty feet from her, a dead man *de seguro.* Yet, in the moment that Huera fired, Tulip tripped her up with her knobbly mesquite walking cane. Down went the Blonde, the rifle blasting harmlessly, and Allison wrested it from her and tossed it to Kaytennae, all in a breath.

Hauling the holy woman to her feet, the Texan barred his arm across her throat, strangling her. If she wanted to taste the air of life again, he rasped in her ear, she would call off her fellow tribesmen now rushing up. He eased his arm, and her voice wobbled forth just in time to slow the Nednhi in their approach to see who had fired the rifle shot. It was then that Allison seized back the Winchester from Kaytennae and yelled for us to run.

Kaytennae went away from there like a rabbit from a burning brush heap. I jumped after him. To my amazement Tulip scuttled along behind us. Overtaking me, she passed young Kaytennae and was first to the rocks, where she gathered in Little Buck protectively. The boy did not care for the embrace but Tulip smacked him a good smack and said, "*Cállate*, shut up," and then yelled down the slope to where Allison was dragging Huera up toward us by her sun-bleached hair, "*Wagh*, Tejano! *Más aprisa*, hombre!" And the Texan, in turn, yelled at the Apache pressing him to hold back or he would blow out the soft belly of their warrior woman with her very own "Yellow Boy" Winchester rifle.

The threat worked to get him and the woman safely into the rocks with us. It was here that I panted to him under-breath that Kaytennae had told me he knew a secret way to go by foot down off the mesa. Allison only nodded, "That's fair good news, Padre; stay down," and levered the brass-framed Winchester to throw a shot at our pursuers who were coming on again.

At this point there were some forty Nednhis in the group that had followed Allison and his "holy shield" into the higher rocks at timber's edge. On the warning shot, they slowed and spread a bit but did not stop. The Texan fired three more rounds, the bullets whining away into the night from the rocky slope, deflected and screaming wickedly. There were two yells, as from hits, and the wailing cry of a woman, and the Apache scattered back and took cover.

"Old Kaytenny," Allison said, "get set to lead

your first war party. On *foot,* hombre." He exploded two more ricocheting shots among the Nednhi. "*Ugashe—!*"

And so we went up and out of the amphitheater of the rancheria basin, into the mesa forest.

The Nednhi came after us, of course.

There was no moon yet and we were not on a traveled trail. Kaytennae followed a pathway of sorts, but we who came behind him suffered frequent and noisy collisions with stump and stone, standing tree and down. It made our tracking a matter of "listening us out" and no people on earth hear more keenly than the Apache.

So we ran a patterned flight of going a desperate pace for so far, then halting to freeze in place and listen intently to locate the pursuit.

It was during the third of these dangerous delays that we heard Juh puffing up to join the momentarily halted searchers and, directly after Juh, we could distinguish the clear voice of Robert Flicker who took advantage of the pause to officially, and smartly, restore the warchief to his command by saying, "You are the leader, Jefe. What will we do?"

Juh suggested total pursuit but when someone informed him his first wife was with the fugitives, he roared out, "What? You expect me to hunt down my own woman? Fools! And you, black one! *You* ask *me* what we will do? I will tell you. Nothing. They can't escape. There is only one way down off this mesa of mine. All know that!"

The logic was Apachean. And Robert Flicker, realizing the truth in Juh's rhetoric, sided with him.

"The warchief is right, brothers," he said. "Let them go. The people can run them down tomorrow. For ourselves, we cannot wait longer. We must be gone for Casas Grandes tonight."

Otsai, the killer, held back.

"What of Huera?" he demanded to know.

Flicker replied that we would never harm the holy woman as she was our hostage. As well, the Blonde had her sacred power to protect her. Might one lame blackrobe priest, with a humped back and no *cruz* with him, offset the medicine of a Nednhi *gouyan-kân*?

Allison and I leaned together, nearly bursting our ears to hear Otsai's answer. It was not good.

He still wanted to go after us. But Juh sided angrily with the Negro deserter, and it grew ugly. Flicker needed some "medicine" of his own, and Tubac gave it to him. "Listen, brothers," Flicker began, stalling for an inspiration, "we must go and cut off those supply wagons before they come up to Casas Grandes. That is the big part of my plan. Why, those wagons—"

He was interrupted by Tubac smiting himself on the forehead and calling out, "*Ahai*! the wagons! I just remembered a thing about the wagons. Jee-le, Ruiz's wife, told us. There's a soldier cannon with them."

"My God," said Robert Flicker softly.

And I heard Ben Allison, lying beside me with his hand over Huera's mouth, utter a harsh Texas oath.

Now, suddenly, all was changed.

With that piece of field artillery in Apache hands and a West Point Academy soldier to operate it, the horse soldiers in my mission were doomed. Flicker could mount the cannon to fire into the garden, and the Nednhi riflemen, stationed on the desert all around the adobe perimeters, would execute any Yanqui trooper coming over the walls to escape the explosions of the fieldpiece inside the garden.

Explaining this to his followers now, the black sergeant finished, "It will be like shooting agency beef cattle in a corral, brothers. Ysun has sent us this great gun. It is the same gun that defeated Cochise in Apache Pass. Our god has given it to the Chiricahua now. It is his sign to us. It is the plan, brothers. *Ugashe*—!"

This time they went. All of them. Yelping and crying at Flicker's heels like so many red wolves hot for the blood of white horse soldiers caught in a trap.

"Christ Jesus," said Allison. "I've seen them use that artillery piece at the fort. If Flicker gets that cannon, he'll chew up them horse troops in five minutes. We got to do something, Padre, and *pronto*!"

Unconsciously, he eased his grip on Huera. The woman drew sucking breath to scream. Like a pit viper from the dark, Tulip, hearing the intake of breath, swung her cane at the Blonde. The blow caught Huera just below the breasts, athwart the solar plexus, paralyzing breath and voice. Tulip poked Ben Allison with the end of the mesquite stick. "Put something in her mouth, Tejano. Or I will knock off her head."

"I believe you, mother," Allison said, and he used his red Texas kerchief to gag the holy woman. Handing the Winchester to Kaytennae, he added, "Hombre, you're in charge. I'll be back by moon-up." He was gone before I might say anything. Kaytennae, however, spoke. He put the muzzle of the rifle into his aunt's ear and murmured in Apache, "If you move *gouyan-kân*, *zas-tee*."

What he had said was that if the wise holy woman made him do it, he would simply kill her.

Huera, neither then, nor later, said a word.

But she knew her adopted nephew.

And she did not move until tall Ben Allison shadowed back in out of the moondarkness and said, "Coast is clear, Padre. The Apaches are all down in camp fixing to ride out. Nobody hid out to tail us. It's meeting time. Kaytennae, where at is this 'hole' of yours?"

"Not far, Al-li-sun."

"Padre, I want you to take Little Buck and go with Kaytennae and the others."

"Wait!" I cried. "What of you, Allison?"

"I got to get down off this rock the fastest way there is," he answered, as if there were nothing more to it than the bare words, "and the fastest way there is, is by the cliff trail. Now once down off the cliff, happen any outhouse luck clings to me, I can beat Flicker and his 'Paches to Casas Grandes and clear them poor damned soldier boys out of there in time. But first off, I got to beat the bastards to the cliff trail." He turned to Kaytennae. "Gimme the rifle, hombre."

The young Apache surrendered the gun and Allison started off. But Kaytennae called after him, "There is only the one thing, Tejano; it is already too late over there. Don't you see the lights moving?"

Allison stopped short. We all came forward to where he stood. Off through the pines we could see the torches of the people going on foot with the departing mounted warriors into the distant U-notch.

"*Lo siento*," murmured Kaytennae. "The trail is shut."

Quietly, Allison agreed. "Only your hole in the rock left, old Kaytenny," he said. "Everybody move out."

At once, Tulip refused. "I have heard of that

hole," she said. "I won't go down it; and this one," she kicked Huera brutally, "isn't strong enough. But I will tell you something, big Tejano. I like you. You may think I am too old, but I am not. And once I was beautiful, did you know that? *Anh*! My mother called me Antelope Child. Isn't that pretty? Anyway, the hell with that. I want you to get away, and I brought some things for you in case you beat Juh down there with the lances."

She stood up and shook off her voluminous blanket. The moon was peering among the pines now and we all saw the amazing store of articles carried beneath the bulky cover. There was Bustamante's Walker Colt and full belt. Also the *alcalde*'s two wicked-looking butcher knives. And Allison's horsehair riata stolen from the same mayor's *casa.* And one more thing: the Spanish slave iron and chain removed from Little Buck.

Faster than any of us might reply, Tulip had flung the slave collar about Huera's bronze neck and toggled the free end of the chain to a jack-pine sapling. Tapping the heavy mesquite cane on the holy woman's back, Tulip said to Ben Allison, "Go ahead. I will stay here and hit her like a damn pack mare if she makes one squeak. Don't worry about me. When the holy one and I have spent this night together, we will both be beautiful."

Ben Allison went to the homely elder wife of the warchief and said, "*Mujer linda*, don't tell

Juh," and implanted a resounding kiss full on the lips of Antelope Child. "*Hasta la vista*," he waved, and he and I and Little Buck went swiftly off through the forest following Kaytennae.

Positively the only thing said further of parting came from the Texas boy, recovering for his first words since being dumped in the rocks by tall Ben.

"Cripes," announced Little Buck Buckles. "There ain't been this much fun since me and Toadie Burnet smoked old Miz Tarberry outen the crapper at Prairie Star school. You should have seen her go without them bloomers to bother her stride. Tarnation—!"

31

While Kaytennae led us the short distance to the secret "mouth of the Pipe," he told us his story of discovering the "other way down."

He had been hunting alone one day with a new rabbit bow Juh had made for him on his twelfth birthday. He had gotten lost in the timber on a part of the mesa where he had never been. Suddenly, a puma kitten, also seeming to be lost, leaped from the brush nearby where Kaytennae rested. When the Apache boy moved toward the baby mountain lion, it ran. Kaytennae gave chase.

After a long run, the cub went into one end of an

old downed cedar log that had become petrified with the centuries. It lay abutted into the shelf from whence it had toppled, and Kaytennae, crawling into it after the mewing kitten, could, strangely enough, see a dim light beyond. Going toward the light, he came into the very stone of the mesa itself and found there a large room as big as an Apache beehive jacal. This was the mouth of the Pipe.

But the lion cub was gone. Tracking the cub in the dim daylight that filtered from a crevice in the mother rock far, far overhead, Kaytennae followed the small footprints on the smooth sand of the cavern's floor. On the far side was a big rock and behind the rock began a long decline—like the stem of a ceremonial clay pipe—boring downward into the mountain at a gentle slope. Kaytennae went down it a long way, but then he thought he heard the growls of the cub's mother, and he climbed up again and out through the petrified cedar tree and home to Juh.

When he told his story to the warchief, Juh said the lion cub was a positive sign from Ysun that Kaytennae should become the tribal bearer of the secret of the Pipe. Juh then said that only he knew the location of this "other exit" from his stronghold, and that Kaytennae, after the Indian way, must keep its secret until he passed it on to his own son, in his own time.

Kaytennae had never been back to the Pipe, but

Juh had told him how it went on from where he had turned back when he heard the lion's growls. Now, they would all have to trust him to remember what the warchief said. "And look!" he finished, pointing ahead in the moonlight. "A good omen to begin with; there is the old stone cedar, exactly as I recall it to be."

We stumbled forward, Little Buck, Ben Allison, and I, not believing yet the reality of such a tale.

But there it was, the petrified downed cedar log.

And into the end of it we went, and on along its hollowed center on hands and knees until, *de pronto*, we broke free of it into the cavern of the mouth.

"Christ Jesus," breathed tall Ben Allison. "Even moonlight shines into it. It's eerie as hell."

"Gives a feller the fantods," shivered Little Buck. "Let's get agoing."

"Down into the stem there is no light to follow us," Kaytennae said. "But Juh told me there were tallows here, not of Indian kind. Do you have matches, Al-li-sun?" He sought with his fingers along a ledge above the portal rock of the stem. Directly, he found what Juh had said he would find. I could not believe it when Allison scratched a stick-sulphured match and I saw the tallows of the warchief's story.

They were of the manufacture of the Church dating two centuries and more into the past. I would guess them to be made by the Jesuits of

Sonora, possibly for the legendary Lost Mines of Tayopa, and stolen by Indian miners from whom the Apaches had secured them.

"*Santissima! qué maravilla*!" I murmured.

Allison put his match to one of them. It caught and smoldered, then burst into a good clear flame—after two hundred years! "Mary save us!" I cried.

The Texan peered across at me in the shifting aurous light. "Ain't nothing against Mary, Padre," he said, "but seems to me this save is on old Kaytenny."

I opened mouth to admit the credit due the Apache youth, but the boy was quicker than I, denying it.

"No, Al-li-sun," he said. "Juh is the one."

"Juh, hombre?" The Texan squinted.

"Think about it," the young warrior said.

Allison frowned hard, and of a sudden the pale eyes widened and the dark face brightened. "By God, Padre," he said, "the kid's right. When Juh turned them back from us by saying there was only one way down off the mesa, he knowed of this other way, and knowed Kaytenny knowed it. I don't get it, but I ain't augering it; that Injun wanted us to get away."

"He did it for the white boy," Kaytennae said. "And for me."

"For Little Buck? For you?" I was truly puzzled.

"Yes, Blackrobe. Juh believed he owed you for

my life. That calls for another life returned. He has just given you that life—the Texas boy."

"Cripes," said Little Buck. "He *did* like me."

Ben Allison took the second of the three ancient torches and lit it from the first one. He passed the new light to Kaytennae and started to put the third, unlit torch inside his shirt front.

"No," the Apache youth said. "Leave one."

It was the Indian way, and Comanche-reared Ben Allison understood. Something is always left for those who follow. "*Enjuh*," he said to Kaytennae and put back the unused tallow. "Lead out, we're way late."

So it came to pass that a Nednhi Apache boy led three strangers down through the mighty rock of Juh's Stronghold, twelve hundred feet by the pipestem—a descent to be remembered in nightmares for a man's lifetime—out into the inner ranges of the Sierra Madre of the North and over them by goat and coyote trails to the other drainage and so, at last, on midday of the second sun, out upon the ancient Chiricahua trail of South Way—not one mile distant from Old Campground!

We were all achingly weary and sore of foot, but when we came out on that old Apache track and young Kaytennae told us where we were, our spirits were restored. Allison said, "By God, we still got time to head them to Casas Grandes. Come on." Little Buck Buckles yelled out, "That's so, old Ben. Yee-hawwhh!"

Kaytennae glanced at me. "Blackrobe," he grinned, "I think you are glad now that you cured me of the horse fever. *Ugashe*, Padre, I am proud of you, too."

He had never called me padre in his life, and I went with him and Ben Allison and Little Buck down out of the rocks and into the main roadway of South Way, the historic Apache trail to Pa-gotzin-kay, feeling in some manner as if my priesthood and my preaching mission in this remote *monte* of my mother's dusky people had, at long last, borne fair fruit.

I was ready, as I am sure were my fellows, to thank a just and generous Maker for delivering us from the Apache wilderness. Indeed, I had just expressed this sentiment to Allison, trudging along at his side in the warm midday dust of the trail, when Kaytennae suddenly stopped ahead of us. In three more strides we were up to him, seeing what he saw: we had walked happily into a trap.

There, just beyond a rocky turn, sat a score of Indian horsemen. They were Apaches, and, more than that, Apaches known to Kaytennae.

"*Enjuh*," said our young guide, raising his right hand to the leader of the silent pack. "I am glad to see you again, uncle. How have you been?"

The man so addressed was a frightful-looking fellow. Of medium age and stature, he was horribly disfigured by some accident of war or of the hunt—we later learned he was torn nearly asunder by a grizzly bear—and when he now smiled in response to Kaytennae's greeting, his face seemed one great, reopened wound. I shivered in the broad day and hot sun.

"Well," he said, "I think the real question is *where* have you been, nephew of the Nednhi."

With that, he waited. His followers' only movement was to nod their heads in agreement to what he said.

"These are my friends, uncle," said Kaytennae, gulping hard. "Here is Blackrobe Jorobado, from Casas Grandes. There is the Tejano, Al-li-sun, a quarter-blood Comanche whose grandmother was own-sister to the father of the great Quanah Parker. And this is his little son, by a white woman," he lied, in concluding. "We are on a little journey going down to Casas Grandes, and I became confused and took the wrong turn. I can't imagine how I got on South Way, starting from Old Campground."

"Neither can I, boy."

"Well, uncle, how are all my cousins among your Warm Springs people? How is my uncle Victorio? And old Nana? You know, the Nednhi think that I am a Warm Springs. Did you ever hear that?"

"Boy," said the disfigured chief, "you're a poor liar. Just like Juh. And your manners are no better than his. You haven't introduced me to your friends."

Kaytennae made a nervous laugh.

"Oh," he said to us with a futile little wave, "*lo siento mucho.* This is my uncle Loco."

Allison and I looked at one another.

Loco—! The craziest of the crazy. God's name!

"Padre," Ben Allison said to me from the side of his mouth, "what were you just saying about thanking the Lord? Cancel my share of the ceremony. Jesus!"

Loco made a sign to his warriors and they swept around us on all sides, and Loco pointed with his rifle toward Old Campground and said, "*Ugashe.*"

And that is how we came back to Old Campground, the comrades three: Alvar Nunez, Ben K. Allison, and Henry Garnet Buckles III.

32

When Juh and Robert Flicker led the big war party out of the stronghold it marked the third time only in all Nednhi history that horsemen had gone down the great cliff by night. But Ysun was with the venture. The descent was made without loss of man or animal, and minutes before midnight the party was on the floor of Cañon Avariento. The moon of course was virtually day-bright, and the little Apache horses knew each rock and step and *sinuoso* in the track. They were across the divide, out of Sonora back into

Chihuahua, by noonhalt next day. Traveling only with resting times for the ponies, the party was in Old Campground by 6:00 a.m. the second day. Here, to save something of their war mounts, the Nednhi stopped four hours to water and graze the little animals and catch a wolf nap for themselves. Thus it was that when Loco and the Warm Springs raiders, coming up from Pa-gotzin-kay, found us in the trail and took us with them on to Old Campground, we found the pony droppings of Flicker's band still warm and smoking.

We found more than that, also.

Four old friends were there.

There were two of them chasing the other two. The warriors of the committee, Sunado and Keet, were trying to catch up two fresh mounts for their own old ponies who had gone lame on the forced march, causing the two men to stay behind when the Nednhi pushed on for Casas Grandes. And the two fresh mounts were Tin Can and Mean Trick, my twin hinny mules. Missing us in the melee atop the mesa, they had followed the war party down the great cliff sniffing the airs of home with each mile over West Way toward Casas Grandes.

Now the little ones had just come upon the stranded war party members and were trying to get around them and go on home down past the Nednhi Falls. Keet and Sunado were cursing and throwing rocks and *hoh-shuh-ing* and coaxing the mules by turn. Allison and I surely would have laughed to see this display of cunning and good taste by our small friends the hinny twins except that the presence of the two Nednhi was very poor medicine for us. It meant that Loco would be informed in detail of Juh's mission in Casas Grandes, instead of hearing the lies we had planned to tell him when we saw that the big war party had already passed through Old Campground. But Kaytennae, quick in the mind, as always, beat them to it.

"Uncle," he said to Loco, the instant we saw the abandoned Sunado and Keet chasing Tin Can and Mean Trick, "I forgot to tell you something; Juh and the black soldier took a big party down from the stronghold to attack some soldiers in Casas Grandes. See, there are Keet and Sunado. They will tell you."

What Keet and Sunado had to tell Loco was that nephew Kaytennae was a traitor and a liar, that the white boy was the own and only son of the *gobernador* of all of the state of Tejas, and that the black sergeant-soldier had sentenced both the priest and the tall, pale-haired Tejano to die for their efforts to free the boy and cheat the Nednhi out of the great ransom of new seven-shooter rifles from Post of El Paso. More than that, also. If Loco and his twenty fresh men would care to go on to Casas Grandes and help in the horse soldier shooting, Juh was certain to reward them with a share of the Spencer guns.

What had Loco to say to that?

The comment of the Warm Springs subchief was an echoing "*Wagh*!" Someone back in the ranks of the Warm Springs fighters shouted out, "*Ugashe*!" And, *de pronto*, the entire party of us was strung out on the run past Laguna de Luz going for the Nednhi Falls and the home trail down into the canyon of the Casas Grandes.

I remembered that return to Old Campground for one thing—the pure fault of Little Buck Buckles.

As we went by the white sand beach I was straining to look away from it. But the damnable boy called out, "Hey, Reverend, looky there! Jesus! Did you ever see such a passel of ants acoming outen only two dinky holes?"

I looked, may God forgive the sight.

But He never will.

The "two holes" of Little Buck's delighted outcry were the places where the scalpers' heads had been before the *lobos* came, now coal-black with the swarming millions of carnivorous soldier ants dining endlessly on what the wolves could not reach.

"Wicked boy!" I shouted. "Shut up and hang on to my cowl, or you will bounce off. For a *peso*, I would give you an elbow and knock you off on my own part."

For once, he subsided.

And indeed even for a wiry boy it was no mean

act to stay with Tin Can on that rocky trail. The Warm Springs people had put the boy and myself on the one hinny mule and big Allison—bound securely—on Mean Trick, the other, stronger twin. Neither little beast would be left behind by the Apache ponies and when, shortly, we went "over the edge" at the Nednhi Falls, our Spanish *mulitas* caught us up easily with the war party's mad spirit to race the daylight for Casas Grandes.

33

We came up with the Juh party and Robert Flicker just at sundown. The meeting was in the higher roughs below the mouth of the canyon of the Rio Casas Grandes. Before us, quiet in the calm of the late afterglow, lay the pink-dusty town and, off to our right upon its separate rise, my "deserted" Mission of the Virgin.

But it was not deserted.

Bivouacked within the adobe walls of my courtyard and garden was the scout company troop of Lt. Jefferson Flowers. Forty men, four corporals, two sergeants, four Lipan Apache enlisted scouts, and, most ominously significant, *no supply wagons.*

The Indians caught Flicker's excitement over this discovery. One could feel the animal sense of the kill stirring the intent ranks of dark horsemen. It was a wind-still evening and, in the clear green light of the desert's departing day, we could all see, off to the north about ten miles, the low dust-sign lying over the old river road to Janos. The wagons. And with them, *a ciencia cierta*, the artillery cannon.

A military council ensued.

Juh and Loco sat as equal chiefs, but both listened to Robert Flicker whose hour it clearly was.

The main parties, Nednhi and Warm Springs, dismounted. The ponies were led back higher yet into the roughlands and picketed there. In itself, Allison whispered to me, this was disturbing. Indians almost never "tied up" their horses. We were going to see a real "blood fight," the Texan told me.

The ponies sequestered, the warriors spread into the nearby rocks, breaking into small groups to rest and eat. A central corps of the most dangerous fighters stayed with the high command in council. This number included several individuals known to us from the Nednhi: Sunado, Keet, Tubac, Ka-zanni, Nazati, Bèle, Tislin, Delgete, Kaytih, and Doce. Otsai, having the all-important charge of the horse herd, was not present. For the Warm Springs, I knew four: Tzu, Vaquero, Tasati, and Mendez, all "bad ones."

Allison and I, under guard, the Texan still bound, were, for reasons of Flicker's insistence, permitted to remain. This puzzled me, but Allison, with his unclouded simplicity, saw through it immediately. The renegade Negro wanted witnesses, he said. And not Indian ones. A Mexican priest and a Texican white man were just about as good as a black man gone bad could hope for. That is, if Ben Allison was right and Robert E. Lee Flicker had it in his touched mind that he was that night entering the Chihuahuan history.

"Why, then, praise God," I whispered, "that means they do not intend to kill us."

"It ain't us we got to worry about," came the Texas-drawled return. "It's Kaytenny and the kid. Did you see where at they got to? The bastards had me down in the dirt on my face; I couldn't see nothing."

"Otsai took both of them with him, up the river with the horses. They'll be safe there."

"With crazies nobody's safe nowhere. Now you listen and you listen hard, Padre. You still got those two butcher knives old Tulip give us up to the mesa?"

I felt beneath my robe and told him, yes, they were yet there, the Apaches had not searched me. He then instructed me to stay as near to him as I might and, when he gave the word, to cut him free. If, meanwhile, we were separated by the Indians, I was to get to Kaytennae and free him, if I could, as he would then be the last, best chance for Little Buck and myself.

Before I could assure him of my understanding and willingness, one of our guards, a squat monkeylike Warm Springs stranger, saw us whispering and came over and struck Allison repeatedly with his quirt. Sunado heard the disturbance and came over from the meeting. When the Warm Springs man told him that the blackrobe and the Tejano were talking too much, Sunado ordered Allison taken away. The last I saw of him, they had roped his feet and were dragging him off up into the rocks, helpless on his back.

Alone, I returned fearful gaze to the council.

Even as I did so, it was breaking up. The decision had been taken. The Apaches would go for the big gun.

Flicker ruled that, as premier chief, Juh must remain in command of the base camp. Even I could see this was a device to free the black sergeant of his unpredictable ally. But Juh had lost kinfolk in the artillery killing among Cochise's band, and he was still supremely a wild Apache, hence deeply apprehensive as to soldier cannon. He made no objection to remaining at the camp, except that he wanted his nephew Kaytennae to go along that the youth might learn how to steal the big guns. Flicker had to remind him that the boy was prisoner to Otsai and must, as a risk to the entire plan, remain so until battle's ending.

Juh admitted the need, and Flicker swept on.

With Flicker would go Loco and the ten Nednhi fighters then present. The Warm Springs chief had far greater experience with white men than any other Chiricahua hostile. He had spent more time on the Americano reservations, San Carlos, Ojo Caliente, Tularosa, Rinconada, all of them, than the rest of the four bands together. So he would be the logical Chiricahua to go with Flicker after that big gun with those white soldiers up on the Janos road. Again, Juh agreed. Knowing the fierce pride and wild heart of the big Nednhi, I could scarcely accept his compliance. But wild Indians are the most sensitive of God's man-creatures. Like wild horses, they are easily hurt by any surrounding of their freedoms. And I knew that my dangerous friend, the warchief, was, in that moment of "going for the big soldier gun," feeling within
his savage breast the mustang's nameless fear of entrapment by the brushwings of the corral that he cannot see but knows instinctively is there.

I prayed hard then that Juh would see, before it was forever too late, that his corral was Robert Flicker. That Juh would suddenly witness the light, resume command of his people, and drive out the black usurper.

God was elsewhere that spring evening.

Within minutes of council's close, Flicker and Loco, with their ten-man picked war party, were riding for the Janos road.

34

Flicker and his Apache raiders were back within four hours. They had the big gun. And more. Ysun had ridden with the Indians. Only two wounds had been taken, by Tislin and Delgete, neither serious, and all of the soldiers with the wagons and the guns were dead. Not one left alive to bear the news to Lieutenant Flowers that his soldier cannon was gone. Even the wind had been kind; it had come up to blow stiffly along the river, northward, carrying from the site of the wagon attack all the sounds of rifle and pistol shooting in the brief massacre.

Robert Flicker showed me the captured cannon.

We pushed through the Apache curious, six and eight warriors deep, about the mighty weapon. I noted that none of the Indians would touch the cannon but that all were intensely stimulated by its presence. The Negro sergeant told me he himself had had to guide the four-mule artillery hitch to move the fieldpiece. I did not need to be told the rare skill required to get that great rifled gun into the roughland rocks from the Janos road, unassisted. By then I knew Robert Flicker's genius. This driven man, given any decent fortune and common kindness of brother man, *would* have been in the American history books not those of Chihuachua. Yet fate, cruel and relentless, had flawed the fine mind, perverted the remarkable gifts.

R. E. L. Flicker, barring intervention of Providence, would lie in the lost grave of human injustice with his father, Black Jim.

No priest of the faith could fail to suffer these spiritual glooms in the Apache camp above Casas Grandes that evil night before the dawn that would signal the shelling of his beloved *Misión de la Virgen de Guadalupe.* The seethe of activity to emplace the cannon admitted no lesser despair. One knew, even though but a soldier of the cross, that the new day would bring not only death to good men of both sides, but destruction of his own life's work. There remained no possible escape for the church and its small enclave of court and garden and ancient burial plot. To be certain, I consulted with Flicker. His bearing was sober, his sympathy unquestionable. But I was right; when, with first sunlight, he would commence his firing of the rifled cannon into my ancient mission, he would not halt its barrage while one adobe brick remained to stand upon another.

"Father Nunez," he said, "God will have to judge between us. This vengeance is mine, not His."

I still could not decide his sanity, and cannot yet. But Robert Flicker was a man to remember.

Now my own time of decision came upon me,

interrupting priestly concerns for the moral judgments of men. Ben Allison had left me with a charge. If I knew not where the Texan was, I must seek out Kaytennae and Little Buck. As the night hours fled swiftly, I grappled with this trust. Finally, an hour before daybreak, I asked God to again forgive me and, checking a last time to be sure the knives of Bustamante were yet strapped beneath my robe, I sneaked away from where my two Warm Springs guards had fallen fitfully aslumber.

Almost in the moment that my footsteps faded up the canyon track toward the horse herd's picket lines, I sensed the sudden quickening of the fates that ever seems to funnel the affairs of men to a common end from many separate beginnings.

Why I knew this, *quién sabe*?

It was simply that something told me that all would not run wildly to the finish, and that those of us who would survive the running must run first.

I found the Apache pony herd in the canyon's curve and had the luck of God to find Kaytennae and Little Buck held in the same spot and by a nodding guard. I went directly down the bank of the river and cut Kaytennae free but had only begun to saw upon the Texas lad's bonds when, without warning, the Nednhi youngster bolted from my side into the rocks above the channel.

Next instant I heard a guttural Apache curse

and saw the lean form of Otsai bound after Kaytennae like a red panther. There was not a sound in any of this. But the guards of Kaytennae and Little Buck, five men, the same ones who held the herd under Otsai's command, had the Indian "inner ear" for noises of the night in enemy country. They were awake on the instant and leaping silently to join the Nednhi killer in his pursuit of the nephew of Juh.

Only then was the stillness broken. The breaker, *por supuesto*, was Little Buck Buckles.

"Crimeny, Reverend," he blurted, wiping sleep from rounding blue eyes. "What you doing with that there Mexican toad-stabber? Hey," he looked around the Apache picket line, "where at are all the Injuns?"

It was an excellent question.

For once, I had an equal answer.

"Why," I said, slashing through his ropes, "they've run off into the rocks after your friend Kaytennae, and I suggest you and I do the same thing. Come on, *chico. Más aprisa*!"

The Texas boy was awake now. The blue eyes snapped. "Tuck up your skirts, Reverend," he cried. "Happen you think you're agoing to stay up with me in that there pope-of-Rome suit, you're daft. Thisaway!"

He darted down the canyon, not up it to follow Kaytennae's flight. Since he was my major charge now, I followed him. After one quick fall into the rocks as I tripped on my robe, I hoisted high the garment of my office and fled, with Little Buck, back toward the main Apache encampment and Robert Flicker's ominously pointing "big soldier gun."

If I needed a spur, the Texas boy provided it in the next common leap. "Attaboy, Reverend," he panted, as I gained even with him. "I was feared you might have broke your butt yonder. And I got need for you and that there blade of yourn. Let her out a notch!"

He increased speed and I only recaught him by inspired effort.

"What?" I gasped. "What did you say?"

"Hold onto your knife," he answered, voice held low now. "I know where at they got old Ben Allison. Heard one of these here pony-guard bucks a-telling Otsai abouten it. They didn't know I savvied Mexican."

"Spanish!" I puffed.

"Yeah," he said. "Nor Spanish neither. Rustle your backside, Reverend. We're nigh there."

My impudent, atrocious scoundrel of a guide was correct. After a skid and a hard turn to go, to the right, up an ascending dry tributary to the Casas Grandes, we came upon a level, upper widening of the wash. There we found and, by a miracle, freed Ben Allison. God had provided that the Texan's twain of Apache watchmen had heard the sliding of rocks on the higher slope occasioned by the swift silent hunting of Kaytennae by his own duped guards, and the two had disappeared to scout the sound only seconds before we arrived.

One was to presume they reappeared only seconds after we departed, also. For, even as the three of us scuttled back down the sandy arroyo, we heard the dry rattle of rocks marking their return, then the angry gutturals of their Apache oaths to find their prisoner cut free and gone.

"Lay low!" Ben Allison hissed and pressed both Little Buck and me back into a shallow indenture behind a gnarl of desert piñon. Next moment, the two Apaches hurtled by, down-gully, growling in their rage. Only when they were safely gone did the big Texan lift us up from the rock and sand and say, in that dusty-dry, San Saban drawl, "Well, Padre, we're back in your bailiwick. You got any bright ideas on where two Texas boys might hole up in a Mexican parish? Just for a couple of days, till the rangers gets here."

I knew it was but his Texas way of reassuring the boy and me. I was grateful for it, but the damnable upstart ignored it.

"Listen, old Ben," he said, "we got fust to help out old Kite, ain't we? Wouldn't be none of the three of us a-standing here augering it, wasn't for him."

I quickly told the Texan of Kaytennae's dire peril higher on the slope. Allison nodded frowningly. "I reckon you're right, Bucko," he said to the governor's red-haired heir, "but if we're going to get to Kaytenny, we're going to have to do it powerful quick."

He gestured toward the rock-studded expanse of the higher ground.

"Yonder comes the sun, boy. She's agoing to be broad day in five minutes."

We looked, and it was true.

On the slope, the upper rocks were just being tipped by the red sunlight of the new day. There was already enough illumination, even on the lower slope, to make out Otsai and his fellows prowling like *lobos monterías* for scent, or sight, of the escaped youth.

It was then that Kaytennae did his very brave thing. We could only believe that he did it in hope to save Apache lives—to stop the war before the black soldier started it with the big gun—for to think the young warrior would do it to spare the trapped American troops is to be utterly ignorant of the Apache way.

Suddenly, from the high rocks, up there where the sun had already arrived, the stabbing flashes of a helio mirror lanced down toward the bivouac of soldiers at my mission. Otsai and his hunters saw the bright rays of the signal and gave cry. Down below, the American troops were running from their blankets to evacuate the center of my compound. We could hear their confused shouts, see their ant-small forms race to clear the center area, to get to the shelter of the mission walls. In the same instant, we saw the belching flash of the cannon directly below us and heard the whining shriek of the first big shell sent hurtling into *Misión de la Virgen.*

The explosion of the preaimed shot was precisely on its target, the center of the compound. Had not Kaytennae's helio mirror given the warning, all of the command would have been shredded as they slept. For it was a canister shell, one of the dreaded "grapeshot" loads of the recent American Civil War. And its terrible charge of laterally dispersed metal would have withered all life within my now shattered garden. As it was, the Yanqui troops had survived largely unscathed, and, even as Flicker sent the second round crashing down on them, they were spreading themselves yet more behind available cover of adobe brick rubble.

For that moment, Kaytennae, the nephew of warchief Juh, had saved the white command at Casas Grandes. But who was to save Kaytennae from the command of the killer Otsai, up on the rocky slopes above?

The third and fourth and fifth rounds, even, of Flicker's cannonading of the mission cried away in high wailing arc to explode below, while we crouched in helpless witness to the running down of Kaytennae. The Apaches had jumped the Nednhi youth, now, and were driving him as a rabbit by dogs. And Otsai, of a sudden taken by the *hesh-ke*, the craziness to kill, was firing his rifle at the boy.

"He means to kill the kid," Allison said harshly.

I sensed that the Texan was going to Kaytennae's aid, and I clutched his arm. "You can't reach him," I cried. "And we have the governor's boy here. We might save him, Allison." My voice broke in anguish. "Ah, God! if only poor Kaytennae could reach us!"

"Well, what if he could?" demanded Little Buck in belligerent interruption. "We'd still have to spy us out a hole to lay up in, just as old Ben says. And, why hell's fire, it would have to hold all three of us, too!"

"Yes!" Allison shouted joyfully. "And old Kaytenny makes four! You have hit the jackpot, kid!"

Allison wheeled upon me, the pale eyes blazing. "Christ Jesus, Padre, we *got* us a hole! Don't you remember how you got us out past the walls down yonder?"

Every nerve in my body jerked wildly.

Nombre Dios! yes, I did remember.

In leaving the mission originally, in order to avoid my parishioners who had come up to prowl the Mexican dead, I had guided the Texan underground through the ultimate mission tunnel that exited in the old dry well of the first Franciscans, in the bottom of the narrow Arroyo

Arido, up-slope of the Church of the Virgin.

I seized the hand of Little Buck, and was ready to lead the dash for the lower slope, when the low voice of Ben Allison ordered me to "hold up."

I thought he had lost his control and was in the well-known shock of battle, for he was whipping off his Texas belt with an energy and haste totally alien to the dangers of our situation. But the sun had marched downward to where we were, now, and the burnished silver buckle of his horseman's belt made a makeshift, if very small, hello of its own. Not too far up the slope from us, the buckle's lancing signals of sunlight struck a dark, desperate eye. We all saw Kaytennae burst from the rocks to come bounding down toward us in a spray of rifle shots from Otsai and his howling packmates. Next instant, the Apache youth was among his friends and we were running for our lives to find the old well in Arroyo Arido, before the Apache rifles found us.

It was a narrow victory.

And dark with blood.

35

The ancient wellhead was a tumble of bleached timbers and adobes buried in thick chaparral. This cover, uncleared the past century, permitted us to reach the "hole" ahead of Otsai's scrambling pack.

I went down first, Allison handing down first Little Buck, then Kaytennae, squeezing his own lank form in last. But he was just too late. Otsai's yelpers saw him going in. Allison ducked down, but he had seen something too: Otsai was wearing the big Walker Colt of Alcalde Bustamante. So when the Nednhi came eagerly brandishing his rifle to show his friends where the game had gone to earth, the Texan seized the leader's ankle and yanked him down into the opening.

Strong as a snake, Otsai broke free and, regaining the surface, shouted his comrades back. But now he had left something with us. It was the big Walker Colt. Allison came up out of the ground with the great revolver bellowing in one continuous roar of discharges. The Apaches tried to get away and for a moment, in the heavy drift of the powder-smoke, I believed they had.

Allison knew better.

"Damn," I heard him say. "One shy."

He was gone out of my sight then and we heard a single booming report—the sixth, last load in the relic Walker—and Allison was back carrying one of the new Winchester rifles. "Otsai's," he said, tossing the gun to Kaytennae, who had come up to my side in the opening. "He'll not be needing it. Let's dig."

The vision of the Indian bodies lying all about in the silent sprawl of their falling places went with me into the hole, and I said to the Texan,

"God's name, Allison. *All* of them?" His answer was a grunt and a curse as he struck his head on a timber. "It had to be," he told me. "Did they leave one soldier boy at the wagon jump to bear the bad news home?"

I understood then. We crawled on, crowding Little Buck who led the way. But when we emerged in my confessional inside the church, Allison was still wrong in his Apache arithmetic. One Indian *had* gotten away.

"Tarnation," announced Little Buck, peering back into the tunnel. "Where at is old Kite?"

Kaytennae was gone. At the last moment the call of his wild blood had proven too strong. He had returned to the Nednhi. "May God protect him," I prayed.

"He don't need God, he's got Juh," the Texan said.

And who could argue with that?

Certainly not Little Buck Buckles. Said the Texas boy, wistfully, "Wasn't it for my maw, I'd purely steal a gun and go with him. Old Kite and me, we was prime favorites of old Juh. The jefe, he tooken me same as he done Kite. We was both sons to him. Now he ain't nobody to teach him the rest of Yeller Rose."

"I reckon," said Ben Allison, "that you will grow outen it. And Juh will somehow recover from the loss." He turned on me, the drawl taking its arid edge. "Padre," he rasped, "stay here inside the church with the kid. Lock him up, if you have to. Just don't turn your back on the little son of a bitch. I don't mean to lose him now. Nor you, neither. Stay low—!"

With that, he was gone out of the church, and Little Buck and I, as one, raced to the narrow windows on the courtyard side to watch his progress.

The shelling outside now had reached its crashing zenith. Some twenty rounds had fallen in and around my mission. What proved to be the final one made a direct hit on the church, seconds after the Texas boy and I left its nave. The roof arch held in its last downcaving from the great bursting jolt, and we only felt the gashes and breath-choking of flying masonry, tile shards, and adobes pulverized into strangling dust.

When we could see, we realized one more round into the building would bring it down about us. Even without that round, the broken-in mass of the roof was creaking and settling as though it might come down at any instant, of its own lodged weight.

I dragged Little Buck through the rubble to the outer room of my quarters. Here I followed Allison's admonition, forcing the boy roughly into the linen alcove and locking him in there, shouting his red-haired head off that he hoped "the Injuns win" and "Juh wipes up the whole of Chihuahua!"

Before leaving the room, I glanced fearfully out the rear window which gave sight on the Rio Casas Grandes roughlands and Flicker's cannon.

The big gun stood deserted in its emplacement, blue smoke yet drifting from its fouled and silent muzzle. Off to its right, I saw Robert Flicker running to mount the pony held for him by a knot of Indian horsemen. His tall form was easily recognizable by its much-patched and laundered cavalry sergeant's uniform, his sole garb in the times that I saw him with the Nednhi. He wore it, I will always think, as the badge of his soldier's pride. He could not, in the end, be an Apache. He would die in his old faded blues, honoring the uniform that had dishonored him.

But his cause was still the Apache cause, and he rode now to join the long streams of warriors down the roughland slopes to finish what his "soldier cannon" had shocked and pounded into confusion. In that span of five minutes required for the Indians to race down and infiltrate the gullies flanking the mission, north and south, the doom of the El Paso scout troop of Lt. Jefferson Flowers seemed sealed.

That I might not miss the fate of the Yanquis, I returned back through the still dust-clouded church to the eastern window apertures that gave on the courtyard.

The smoke of gunpowder and exploded adobes lay over all. Great sections of the wall were down. Shellburst craters pocked the court, the garden, the small burial ground. The American soldiers were yet pinned down to the breast-works formed by blown-in walls and cratered earth of the mission garden. As I came again to the church windows, the soldiers were being driven back into these piles of rubble by the riflefire of the Apaches now successfully deployed in both flanking arroyos. There appeared no escape could be made. Flicker's plan of executing the troops like beef cattle in a corral was no longer a nightmare dreamed in Juh's distant stronghold. It was being carried forward at that very hour of the spring morning in my tortured courtyard.

I saw, for a moment where the smokedrift cleared, Ben Allison running up to the sole officer on the far side of the garden. The man was plainly the lieutenant, but he did not seem in command, as the men were being fought by the two sergeants and the corporals. Indeed, he seemed dazed, distraught. I could make that out by Allison's obvious frustration in shouting at him.

But the smoke closed in again. Under cover of this drift-over, a wild-crying rush was made for the walls by the Indians from the gullies. They were repulsed by a brave but thin volley from the perhaps fifteen troopers yet active on each ruined parapet. One did not need a soldier's education to know that the next advance would see the Apaches over the walls.

That charge never came.

I saw, in the final moment of it, Juh's huge form striding the length of the south arroyo. To the north the Warm Springs chief Loco held command, his crippled hunching gait as distinctive to single him out as my own. Both Apache leaders were plainly arousing their fighters for that second, fatal rush. Actually, the Indian charge left both gullies and came on about half distance, when it happened.

There was a blinding stab of light from the roughland high country to the west. A helio mirror was blinding the eyes of the warchief of the Nednhis, and he knew whose slim dark hand held that mirror. The great booming basso of Juh's voice arose over riflefire and soldier shout and war cry of his and Loco's wild-eyed riders. "*Alto*! *Alto*! *Reculamos*—!" And the Indian horsemen, hearing the order to *halt, go back,* wheeled their mounts and drove them for the gullies. Indian warriors will seldom obey in the field as these did that day outside my ruined mission walls. But these Indian warriors knew those mirror flashes as well as Juh did, and there were those of them in both arroyos who could read the urgent sun messages of the looking glass.

That was Kaytennae up there in the hills; and his warning light-stabs told Nednhi and Warm Springs, alike, the same startling war news: *Many enemies coming. Very close. From the east.*

De seguro, Father Alvar Nunez read those words as well as any Apache. Who had taught the Nednhi boy to use the mirror in the first place? *Ay de mí*!

I ran headlong again to my study. I had an ancient pair of Spanish field glasses there. Yet even as I ran the better thought caught up with me—in the bell tower of my caving church reposed a German telescope, used for long-range spying-out of Indian approaches to our mission, originally emplaced there by the Franciscan builders. The tower, by God's grace, was intact. Up its winding well I sped and seized up telescope.

The distant haze of mirage above Big Dry Wash muddied the glass for the first moments, then the image steadied. Coming from the wash, and for the rising knoll of *Misión de la Virgen de Guadalupe*, was a vast company of riders. There was no mistaking the manner of their horsemanship and the nature of their heavy armament—each man with twin revolvers strapped about waist, rifle in hand, and riding like white Comanches. These were Texas riders. And more than that. They were *los Tejanos Diablos.*

Those were the Texas Rangers coming!

Below me, I saw Ben Allison with a rifle hot from firing. "Rangers!" I cried down to him. "It is the Texas Rangers riding out there to the east!"

Hearing me, he ran to the top of the nearest pile

of the wall's rubble, squinting off toward the big wash. "By God, Padre!" I heard him yell back. "You win! And so do we!"

Others were now coming from the walls.

"Rangers! It's the rangers. Thank Christ!"

The men inside and outside the broken walls knew that the fight was over. The Nednhi could see like eagles and the Warm Springs like antelope. They understood, as well, the English cries of "rangers!" and when the great block of horsemen rolled up out of the wash, the Indians in both arroyos were already leaving.

It was in this stark moment that I saw Robert Flicker seize up a loose pony and vault to its back, spurring out of the south gully. But the black sergeant was not going with his departing Apache allies. He was driving the little Nednhi pony through a gaping breach in the mission wall. Then it was that I saw what brought him to this suicidal lone thrust.

It was Lt. Jefferson Flowers.

The young officer was standing almost beneath the bell tower. I could hear him talking to no one. He was completely broken. "The church, Lieutenant!" I shouted down. "For God's sake, run into the church!"

Whether he heard me or ran on fuddled instinct, the officer stumbled up the steps and into sanctuary. Flicker only swerved his mount to follow. Ben Allison shot the small Indian horse out from under the black avenger, full on the incline of the steps. The rider rolled unharmed to his feet, reached the doors, and was inside. I fled the tower, crying to God that He not let the Negro kill his nemesis.

I reached the pews in time to wave back the Texan, running through the door with his rifle, but Flicker already had Jefferson Flowers cornered at the altar.

"Sanctuary!" I cried in low voice to Allison.

And, saying nothing, he stopped with me.

What followed was more destructive to me than the expected slaying. Flowers was crying like a child. He knew he was going to die and he wept and screamed and burbled in his coward's utter agony, to turn a true man's innards. Flicker did not see us behind him. But he was the man that his father Black Jim had made him and had prayed to his God that his son would be.

Flicker turned his back on the sobbing hysteria of the officer and gentleman that he himself could never be, and all the black man said to him, so low and quiet that the Texan and I barely made it clear, was, "God help you."

With that, Flicker turned from the altar and came up the aisle levering his brass-framed Winchester Rifle, prepared to die himself against whatever rush of soldiers would now come pounding on the doors which I had barred behind Ben Allison and myself.

Flicker saw us in the same moment that the soldiers arrived outside the doors, thundering upon them for admittance with their rifle butts. The Negro deserter and the San Saba *pistolero* stood, dark to pale eye, crouched both and each awaiting the movement of the other to kill.

"Robert Flicker," I said, "I give you the right to confession. Will you take it, now, while there is yet time? Our God is the same God. He offers you life Eternal. As you have forgiven your Enemy, thus our God now forgives you. Follow me quickly, my son—!"

The black man hesitated, eyes wild, body trembling.

Allison said quietly, "Do it, Flicker. You don't need to die for nothing. Your war's over."

I took Flicker's arm, and he came with me then. Allison did not once turn our way, but put his back to us and, when I last saw him, he was unbarring the doors of my church and letting the Yanqui soldiers rush in with their rifles at the ready, to execute the black deserter.

But my church stood empty behind the tall Tejano.

No priest, no deserter, not a human thing to shoot down; there was only Lt. Jefferson Flowers to find at the altar and to lead away up the littered debris of the aisle, still sobbing, still mumbling, still pleading for his life.

36

True endings seldom catch all ravels.

When I returned from confessing Robert Flicker, it was in time to see Governor Henry Garnet Buckles of Texas come hero-striding into the ruins of my beloved Mission of the Virgin. He it was who had gathered up the great troop, of mixed "resigned" rangers and general Texas Indian fighters, that had rushed in to "save" the beleaguered army troops "in the very nick of Texas time."

To me it seemed an inequity that this credit went to Governor Buckles, but Allison only laughed and told me not to "fret it." He would settle, he said, for a writ of amnesty from his Honor, clearing him, Ben, of stealing that horse in El Paso. This paper was actually produced by the governor and signed in my presence. I could not believe any reward might be so mean and yet be greeted with such a grin by its receiver. But Allison intrigued me to the end.

He took the paper and waved a proper farewell to Governor Buckles when the governor, who was in Mexico *in flagrante delicto* of the law between his country and mine, gathered up his young son from out the prison of my linen closet, got back to horse with all his men and moved out of Casas Grandes that same afternoon. The army troops went with him. The entire column took the old river road north to Janos, and, by the peace and quietude of the four o'clock evening of the desert *monte*, the last traces of their unwanted dust had thinned into history.

The remove left Allison and myself alone with the poignant awkwardness of two men saying good-bye.

We delayed it to conclude important business in Casas Grandes.

There was the matter of returning, of all things, the twin hinny mules. These little brutes had wandered in off the roughlands after the Apache departure, and Allison, having borrowed them from Bustamante, suggested they be returned with the rest of the missing items to our *alcalde.*

Bustamante was beside himself to see his *mulitas*, which he naturally assumed to have been taken by the Apaches. He insisted that the same criminals had relieved him of the Walker Colt and the two butcher knives of the good Señora Bustamante. What the damnable *indios* had spirited away, the mayor proclaimed, the tall Tejano had retrieved, a miracle surely.

Indeed, nothing would do but that the Texas *pistolero* be given as good as he had brought back.

For the return of Tin Can and Mean Trick, would the señor so kindly accept a very nice *entero* which the *alcalde* had found running loose after the ranger ambush by Juh? The animal came with a good Texas saddle, bridle, rifle, scabbard, *todo.*

Well, what might an honest Texas horse thief do in such a case? Insult the mayor of Casas Grandes? Never. Graciously, Allison accepted back his own stolen horse and, after some toasting in the aromatic cantina of Elfugio Ruiz, the tall man
and the short humpbacked priest went again up the rise to the sunset silences of my ruined mission.

Here we shook hands for the final time.

Allison told me that he believed he would not go home to San Saba immediately but would look around a bit for some people here in Chihuahua to whom he felt an accounting might still be owed.

"There's always somebody left over," he said. "This time it's Santiago Kifer."

I shivered at the memory of the name but nodded my understanding of his need to make the grim search.

"Ride a long life, Tejano," I said, and I stepped back.

Allison swung up on the restless stallion.

"Luck, Padre," was all he said.

But when he and the horse topped South Ridge below Mission of the Virgin, I saw him pause and take something from inside his flat-crowned Stetson. There was enough sun remaining to catch and glitter on the torn pieces of paper fluttering from his hand.

Was it the ransom note?

I never knew.

He rode on, and I could hear his clear, sweet whistling of *The Yellow Rose of Texas* long after the ridge hid him and the stolen El Paso stallion.

Epilogue

The preceding history is not a verbatim transcript of the original *Narrative of Father Nunez.* Rather, it is a selection from that controversial document of material pertinent to the carrying off, from outside El Paso, Texas, circa 1868–73, of young Henry Garnet Buckles III, by certain Chiricahua Apache Indians under Chief Juh. Some detail is thus omitted which ought to have been included. The epilogue attempts to rectify these oversights in that portion of the narrative relating to Nunez's adventures among the savage Nednhi.

The confusion of Apache fortresses in the Mexican Sierra Madre: Pa-gotzin-kay and Juh's Stronghold. Pa-gotzin-kay, said by some accounts to be the site of the rescue of young Buckles, is five days south of Casas Grandes and was not located by white men until the later years of Crook's campaign against Geronimo. Juh's retreat was much nearer Casas Grandes, although it lay in Sonora State, and was generally known throughout the *monte*, due to Juh's habitual travels to the Chihuahuan settlement to trade for whiskey. It is agreed in Chihuahua that the Buckles boy was taken to Juh's Stronghold, "in the Blue Mountains, just west of Cases Grandes two days by a good mule."

Matter of Mexican casualties at Casas Grandes. The Nunez account says the bodies of the federal dead were given mass burial in Arroyo Arido, "to the south of the old wellhead a distance of four hundred *varas.*" Father Nunez administered the rites upon his return from Juh's Stronghold.

The Texas Rangers scalped at Mission Guadalupe: American witnesses. Nunez claims that "a coroner's committee" of noncommissioned officers of the United States scout force from El Paso, and citizens from the invading Texas posse of Governor Henry Buckles, did in fact inspect and certify the ranger dead. There is no con-firmatory record, either in ranger or United States Army files.

The cruz of Father Nunez. The Franciscan Order is said to have the cross that Father Nunez placed above the Texas casualties in his mission garden. However, the order has no comment on any of the Nunez claims, including the very existence of a mission of Saint Francis at Cases Grandes. Like the rangers and the army, the Church does not dignify such *fabulas del monte.*

The related matter of how Misión de la Virgen de Guadalupe, at Casas Grandes, disappeared. It is the severest critique of the *Narrative of Father Nunez* that his church is not remembered in Chihuahua, and that the so-called vestry stones beneath which his document lay buried until 1933 were in fact the masonry floor of an 1885 milking *establo* for the large goat herd of the Rancho Guadalupe, outside the town. Angry defenders of the folklore say there never was a Rancho Guadalupe and no "large goat herd or *lecheria*" out there on the lonely rise where Fr. Alvar Nunez "waited for fierce Juh." Their best story is that the shelling of Robert Flicker's field artillery piece leveled the church, the pastorate, bell tower, the very walls of the garden and cemetery, everything. Through the century that followed, the people of Casas Grandes "used up the rubble" and then, late in the century, the great flood of 1889 undercut the knoll, caved in the site, carried all remaining traces of the ruin away down *Arroyo Arido*, "excepting the vestry stones themselves, which God sheltered from the storm, knowing the treasure they covered."

Why the 1866 Winchester "Yellow Boy" rifles were "new" to the Nednhi Chiricahua. Little understood among aficionados of western history and folklore, is the fact that it was always some years, often a lot of years, before a new design of weapon reached the frontier in numbers. Hence, although the Nunez narrative is dated considerably later than 1866, it is no western wonder at all that such witnesses as Father Nunez and the wild Nednhi were "astounded at the gleaming brass-framed beauty" of the first true Winchester.

The Ruiz Museum of Mexican History. In his cantina, proud owner Elfugio Ruiz for many years maintained a display of memorabilia of the Nunez legend. Among his wares of value were the antiquated Walker Colt, his wife's two butcher knives, the braided horsehair *riata*, the "one and only" genuine "*cruz de Padre Nunez*" and even "Juh's jug," the very one he carried on the day when, drunk, he fell in the Casas Grandes River and was drowned. *Oue tal*! It must be confessed that both Mayor Bustamante and tavern keeper Ruiz were known to get at the mescal a bit early in the afternoon. Yet who really knows? Juh did fall in the river and drown. And an emptied jug was found bobbing in the current downstream. *Enjuh.*

The contradictions of Kaytennae. Like Juh, Kaytennae became a very well-known person in later years. His best biographers insist he was never in the United States until his capture with Geronimo in 1883. This view would rule out his presence with the war party that took young Buckles on the El Paso stage road. But then those same authorities on the Apache—all white men naturally—spell Kaytennae's name six different ways and disagree on his age ten years in two directions and, well, that is only the beginning of the discussion.

Clarification: the four bands of the Chiricahua Apache. There has always been and yet remains a controversy in this matter. White historians tend to consider the four hostile bands, Nednhi, Bedonkohe, Warm Springs, and True Chiricahua as, in fact, all Chiricahuan peoples. Some Indians differ. James Kaywaykla, Warm Springs Apache narrator of Eve Ball's fascinating *In the Day of Victorio*, writes: "I say *peoples,* although the White Eyes designated the members of all four different Apache bands as Chiricahua. This was an error, for only the tribes of Cochise and Chihuahua were true Chiricahua. . . . Juh was chief of the Nednhi Apaches, whose stronghold was in the Sierra Madre of Mexico. Geronimo was leader, but not chief of the Bedonkohes whose territory was around the headwaters of the Gila. Though closely associated, we were distinct groups."

Addendum Kaytennae: his origins. Good and careful white writers on the Chiricahua agree that Kaytennae was a Warm Springs Apache, with no stated record of having lived with Juh and the Nednhi. Given the contentions on the subject, however, as plainly demonstrated above, Father Nunez's claim for Kaytennae's youth being spent among the people of Juh would not appear indefensible. The Apache were a nomad, intermarried people. Blurrings of tribal origins are inevitable.

Later days of Little Buck: what happened to Henry Garnet Buckles III. There is no useful line on the Texas boy. Some say he was wild to the end of his days, which were brief. Some contend he became the gunfighter he thought Ben Allison was. In no event did "Little Buck" contribute to a better society, except that he changed his name to follow the owlhoot trail.

The Spencer seven-shooters: unknown guns that could have won the West. Perhaps this ought to read "that should have won the West." For it is one of the great mysteries of frontier firearms history that Christopher Spencer's great 50-caliber carbine did not go the famous way of the celebrated Winchester. Suffice to say that if Robert Flicker could have seized the weapon in numbers for the Apache, hell would have been spelled Spencer, in Apacheria.

The strange escape of R. E. L. Flicker. No body was ever found for the Negro deserter in Father Nunez's church. The main roof caved the day following the shelling and it was many weeks before the wreckage was cleared in the search for the by-then notorious black soldier. Father Nunez himself is subtle, writing in the *Narrativa* that, "Brave Flicker, one would pray to imagine, yet rides out there in that freedom he did not find with his own people. And who is to say, also, that he did not return to find sweet Huera, his Apache love, and that the twain even now ride the deep Sierra at peace and in happiness, man and woman together?" Knowing Padre Nunez, one may be forgiven that, "sweet Huera" aside, the suspicion lingers that "brave Flicker" was "confessed" right on out the *Arroyo Arido* tunnel, come nightfall and the necessary darkness.

Santiago Kifer and the scalp hunters. There are two elements with regard to Kifer. First, in defending the fact that no corpses were recovered at Old Campground to match the two scalpers he reported slain by Kifer, Nunez says, "It is to be noted that I did not *see* them killed, but only *heard* their murders. Perhaps I was wrong." *Quita*! As for the five Apache bodies said to have been given Nednhi burial at Old Campground, no grave was discovered to explain the absence of those corpses either. But Nunez points out here that nearby the campsite the earth is "riven by the Chiricahua crevice, a splitting of the rock without known bottom," implying of course that Juh simply dropped his dead into this "holy vault."

Addition, S. Kifer and his men. In his *Narrativa*, Nunez appends a grim footnote to the Kifer gang, saying that, "Some days after Allison rode away, a Warm Springs or possibly a Bedonkohe Apache traveling South Way down to Pa-gotzin-kay was stopped by a white man coming up from the south. He had a greasy sack which he gave the Indian, asking only that the traveler see that the sack reached Juh and the Nednhi. The sack was delivered and, according to Jee-le Ruiz, the wife of Elfugio, it contained five heads, all of White Eyes. But the sixth head, that of Santiago Kifer, was not among them and was never found." The implication here is inescapable. But of that element Father Nunez writes, “I do not say and will never believe that the Tejano filled the terrible container.” *Pues, quien sabe*? Perhaps so. Others of the keepers of the Ben Allison *historic* will not be so certain *or* so charitable.

Identification and fate of the “rifled cannon” of Robert Flicker. From Nunez’s sketchy description in the narrative, this was either the M1857 Napoleon 12-pounder, or the M1861 Rodman 9½-pounder, called the “Rodman rifle.” Since it was but two-thirds the weight of the bigger Napoleon, the Rodman would seem to have been the likelier candidate for Flicker’s wild dash up into the Casas Grandes roughlands. If so, the weapon was a 3-incher with a 69-inch tube and weighing but 820 pounds. Its normal rate of fire was two aimed shots per minute, four with canister. This would match the account of the brevity of Flicker’s shelling of the mission—not over ten minutes. The gun was accurate to 1830 yards. Flicker’s range was just over 1000 yards, hence the devastating results. Until the turn of the century, a wheeled carriage was displayed in the plaza in front of *La Cantina Ruiz*, which would have fitted the M1861 Rodman. But the cannon proper had long since been melted down for its barrel’s iron, and in later years the carriage was requisitioned by General Francisco Villa to haul ammunition and *aguardiente* for the revolution. When Ruiz died and the *cantina* burned down the following year, it was not even remembered where the wheels of "Flicker's cannon" had rested.

The Yellow Rose of Texas: its fair words. The lyrics Father Nunez indicates for this old Texas ballad are imprecise. Perhaps it would be more accurate to guess that the Little Buck Buckles variation on the original theme was at fault. The record, at least, is clear.

> She's the sweetest rose of color
> this fellow ever knew,
> Her eyes are bright as diamonds,
> they sparkle like the dew;
> You may talk about your Dearest May
> and sing of Rosa Lee,
> But the Yellow Rose of Texas
> beats the belles of Tennessee.

Casas Grandans old enough to have heard it from fathers who were there insist that Chief Juh frequently performed the number in the plaza on his whiskey trips down from the Sierra, and that he always employed Father Nunez's bowdlerized lyrics; a poetry of some Apachean justice, after all. *Enjuh, Jefe*!

Of the true end of Father Alvar Nunez. It is plain in the inscription of the narrative that Nunez expected Juh and the Nednhi to return for an accounting with him. The priest seems certain of this fate. Yet, as the full manuscript ends, the Apache have not appeared. Did they ever do so? One is permitted to hope, with the same certainty that Blackrobe Jorobado held for Robert Flicker's escape, that, somewhere in all of wide Chihuahua, the lively flesh of Fr. P. Alvar Nunez, O. F. M., wandered the *monte* for many a year in the unquenchable spirit that was his.

About the Author

Will Henry was born Henry Wilson Allen in Kansas City, Missouri. His early work was in short subject departments with various Hollywood studios and he was working at MGM when his first Western novel, *No Survivors*, was published in 1950. *Red Blizzard* (1951) was Allen's first Western novel under the Clay Fisher byline and remains one of his best. As Fisher, he tends to focus on a story filled with action that moves rapidly. His many novels published as Will Henry tend to be based deeply in actual historical events. Under either name, as a five-time winner of the Gold Spur Award from the Western Writers of America, Allen has indisputably been recognized as a master in writing gripping historical novels of the West.

Center Point Large Print
600 Brooks Road / PO Box 1
Thorndike, ME 04986-0001 USA

(207) 568-3717

US & Canada:
1 800 929-9108
www.centerpointlargeprint.com